Heart of the Eagle

by

ELIZABETH GRAHAM

Harlequin Books

TORONTO • LONDON • NEW YORK • AMSTERDAM • SYDNEY

Original hardcover edition published in 1978
by Mills & Boon Limited

ISBN 0-373-02170-4

Harlequin edition published June 1978

PRINTED IN U.S.A.

OTHER
Harlequin Romances
by ELIZABETH GRAHAM

Many of these titles are available at your local bookseller
or through the Harlequin Reader Service.

For a free catalogue listing all available Harlequin Romances,
send your name and address to:

HARLEQUIN READER SERVICE,
M.P.O. Box 707, Niagara Falls, N.Y. 14302
Canadian address: Stratford, Ontario, Canada N5A 6W2

or use order coupon at back of book.

CHAPTER ONE

BRET STAFFORD came back to Gold Valley the day his father was laid to rest in the old hillside cemetery on the edge of the village. But it was not the same Bret who had left seven years before. The earlier Bret had been laughing, happy, bright with the promise of life before him. This one was remote, cold, withdrawn, as if he had experienced all life had to offer and found it wanting.

Or so Jinny O'Brien thought as she looked across the space between her and the bleak-eyed stranger. Grey, now, his eyes were, but she still remembered the warmth of sea green in them when he had teased her and pulled her hair, laughing with strong and even white teeth set in the golden tan of his cheeks.

But that had been long ago, when he was in love with Lesli. Lesli of the golden brown hair and laughing amber eyes, Jinny's older sister who had disappeared one night like one of the wraiths of mist that sometimes enveloped the nearby mountains. Eloped with a man who could promise her more excitement than Bret Stafford could ever offer on a remote wilderness ranch.

Bret's eyes, as if sensing her scrutiny, came up to meet the violet blue of hers and held there a moment, puzzled, before moving with impersonal masculine interest over the rest of her. She buried her neck deeper into the fur-lined parka she wore so that her black curling hair, scarcely contained under a white knitted hat, fell forward over her cheeks. His gaze seemed to pierce the thickness of her jacket and come up with an accurate assessment of her every curve under it.

In spite of the snow floating intermittently in the air,

having a last fling at winter before spring's warmth flooded the Valley, Bret wore only a dark suit, and the white particles settled on his uncovered hair, which was still thick and dark brown. Her fingers still felt that thickness between them, and she grew hot remembering how, at fourteen, she had succumbed to an overwhelming urge to run her hands through his hair one day when he had chased her and brought her down on the sweet-smelling hay in her grandfather's barn. The laughter had faded from his face and he left her abruptly, never to chase her again.

Jinny realised suddenly that the graveside service was over, and that Bret was coming towards her, the puzzled look even more pronounced in his eyes. The dark line of his jacket sat comfortably on his broad shoulders, emphasising the graceful leanness of hips and long legs.

'I feel I should know you,' he said in the familiar voice that sounded like no one else's and sent tremors of remembrance along her nerves, 'but I can't seem to place you.'

'Jinny,' she got out, 'Jinny O'Brien.'

'*Jinny?*' The end of one well-marked brow rose in incredulous disbelief. 'You've—changed a lot! But you must be what?—nineteen, twenty by now?'

'Twenty-one,' she amended quickly. Somehow the difference in age seemed much less at twenty-one and his thirty than it had at fourteen and twenty-three. Not that the confident, obviously successful thirty-year-old Bret would be any more interested in her, a gauche Valley girl, than he had been when she was a girl of fourteen!

'And your grandfather? Is he still——?'

'He would have come today, Bret, but he's been ill and I wouldn't let him. He's—had two heart attacks lately,' she explained hesitantly, not knowing if Bret's inquiry was prompted by politeness or genuine interest. 'I don't like him having too much strain'—she waved a hand vaguely—'such as this would have been, even though——' She caught back the words she had been about to speak, but she might as well have said them for he knew exactly what they would be.

'Even though he and my father were enemies for years!' he finished for her with a bitter smile, then glanced at the gathered handful of mourners grouped some distance away. 'I'm surprised so many turned out on a day like this. My father was never a man to cultivate friendship—even mine!'

'Oh, Bret,' she appealed, her voice low. 'Can't you forget the past and——'

'Some things can't be forgotten, Jinny,' he told her with finality, and changed the subject. 'Your grandfather must have changed a lot, too, if he lets you dictate to him what he can or can't do!'

She flushed. 'Pop doesn't do anything he doesn't want to do,' she said with dignity.

'But you use your female wiles to persuade him that what you want is the very thing he decides to do, is that it?' Bret's smile scarcely reached his eyes, and did little to take away the deep coldness in them. 'Anyway, I'd like to see him while I'm here. Do you think he'd want to see me?'

'Yes—yes, I'm sure he would. He always liked you, Bret.' Indeed, Bret was the only Stafford that Denis O'Brien could bear near him, even before Bret fell in love with Lesli. There was something of an Irish quality in the younger man's exuberant spirits which had endeared him to the man who had left his native shores in physical form sixty years before but whose heart had never left the black peat of Ireland.

'Will you wait for me while I speak to some of the people here?' Bret asked in a voice that seemed to take for granted that she would agree. 'I'll drive you back—or did you drive yourself into town?'

'No, I—I was brought down today.' Involuntarily, Jinny's eyes sought and found Mike Preston's broad figure, easily recognisable in the R.C.M.P. uniform as he chatted quietly with an older man at the edge of the main group of people. Bret's eyes followed hers and his brows rose.

'Your boy-friend's a policeman?'

'He's not my boy-friend,' she denied with a quickening of colour in her cheeks. 'We're—friends, that's all.'

A remote gleam of amusement crossed his eyes. 'He's coming across now, and from the looks of him he's not feeling all that friendly! I'll leave you to break the news that you're driving home with me.'

He turned away just as Mike drew near, a short frown between his pale blue eyes. 'Was that Stafford, Jinny? I wanted to give him my condolences.'

'He'll be back in a minute, Mike. He—he's coming over to see Pop right after he's finished here. Do you mind if I ride back with him instead of you?'

His fair, thick eyebrows went down, deepening the frown. 'I have a couple of hours free, Jinny. I thought we might drive out to that new housing development at Riverview.'

'Oh, Mike,' she sighed, giving him a fretful look. 'You know I can't think of anything like that while Pop's ill.'

'Face the facts, Jinny,' Mike said with an impatient gesture. 'Your grandfather won't be around for ever, and if we could at least look around in the meantime——'

'No! It's like wishing Pop dead to be making plans for after he's gone,' she told him passionately. Acknowledged between them, though never put into words, was her grandfather's antipathy towards Mike or any other uniformed man—a prejudice born in his wild young days in Ireland which nothing Mike said or did could dispel.

'I can't wait for ever, Jinny,' Mike said quietly now, and her eyes sparked with instant anger.

'No one's asked you to,' she flared. 'You've always known I would never leave Pop while he needs me.' She glanced appraisingly round the cemetery where people were beginning to drift towards the gates, and saw Bret shake hands with the men he had been talking to and turn in her direction. 'This isn't the time or place to talk about that, Mike,' she added hurriedly, her heart skipping a beat or two at the thought that Bret, handsome and distinguished-looking in this gathering of local people, was coming specifically to escort her, Jinny O'Brien, to his car.

Contrast was marked between the two men as they shook hands, Mike's fair-skinned face reddened from the tension between himself and Jinny, Bret self-confident though holding himself aloof.

'You're sure the policeman is just a friend?' Bret asked mockingly as he handed her into the passenger seat of the Stafford pale grey station wagon parked just outside the gates. 'If looks could kill, I'd have been dead before I reached the sidewalk!'

He came to open his own door and slide behind the wheel and Jinny said severely: 'That remark was in very poor taste, Bret Stafford, considering you've just——'

'Buried my father? Come on now, Jinny—I've acted the hypocrite for the benefit of those people back there, but I didn't think I'd have to do it for you, too. You know Dad and I never got along, and when my older brother Jack got killed that was the end of his family as far as Dad was concerned.' His long fingers reached for the ignition. 'I guess I was closer to your grandfather than my own father.'

She looked up at him in surprise when he turned to glance over his shoulder, then pull out into the traffic lane. It was Lesli, she had always thought, who had drawn Bret to the O'Brien ranch. Yet as memories trickled through her mind, she recalled long evenings when her grandfather and Bret had played backgammon and chess to a background of Lesli's petulant cries of: 'Bret, you care more about Pop than you do for me!' But he hadn't, of course. It had been left to Jinny to break the news to him that Lesli had eloped with Eddie Clark, a racing driver who had been in the area on a hunting trip for some weeks. Bret's stricken look had haunted her through the years since then.

She watched the movement of his hands on the steering wheel. Although sensitively shaped, they were competent-looking, and less work-hardened than they had been before. He wore no wedding ring, but then many men didn't.

'You—didn't bring your wife with you?' she asked his set profile, her whole world seeming to tremble on the brink of his answer, though she knew it could make no difference one way or the other.

'No, I didn't,' he replied briefly, and sent her heart plummeting only to soar again when he added with a faint sideways smile: 'Mainly because I don't have one.'

'Oh. I thought you—must have married by now.' It was hard to believe that someone as attractive as Bret had not been claimed long ago.

'No. I have most of the benefits of marriage without the encumbrances of wife and children. Does that shock you, little Jinny?' he asked with a glance at her flaming cheeks.

'Yes—no—oh, Bret, I don't know. I've never known anybody who—lived that way.' Jinny turned her head away from him in embarrassment.

'Marriage isn't for me, Jinny,' he stated with quiet finality. 'You know I have a charter plane business out of Vancouver?'

She nodded, remembering the weekly newspaper's write-up about the rapid success of Stafford Air-North, a company started six years before with one plane and pilot—Bret—which had now mushroomed into a fleet of charter planes. 'I still do a lot of the flying myself, and I'm out of town as much as I'm in it. Not many women care to have an absent husband fifty per cent of the time. Besides——' He paused, then went on without changing his tone: 'What do you hear from Lesli?'

'Les——? Oh. Not very much, a postcard now and then. They—travel a lot, all over the world. We haven't seen Lesli since——' In her turn, she broke off and bit her lip, remembering that Bret himself had left Gold Valley the day after Lesli's elopement.

'She hasn't been back to see you and your grandfather?'

'Lesli wanted to, lots of times,' Jinny defended her sister against the censorious note in Bret's voice. 'But with Eddie's schedules, they just couldn't make it. Maybe this summer they will.'

He made no comment to that as they sped by the entrance to Valley Ranch, the Stafford place, its long, low bungalow scarcely visible from the road. Hillside, the O'Brien ranch, lay a further three miles into the Valley, and its seven hundred acres had been a bone of contention dividing the Staffords and O'Briens for fifty years.

Denis O'Brien had followed the stream of gold seekers to the valley that had been named for their quarry, but little had been produced of the precious metal so the prospectors had moved on, leaving Denis to take up the option on seven hundred acres he was convinced held the main seam. The old man was still convinced, despite only an occasional find of small nuggets in the stream that came through his property from the towering mountains behind and led to a picturesque lake where he watered the few cows he ran. Over the years Bret's father, Henry Stafford, had made offers to buy the O'Brien property on the grounds that he needed the watering facilities for his cattle, but Denis was always adamant that Henry was after the gold he knew was there.

Bret's mouth held a faintly ironic smile as he drew up beside the modest frame bungalow that had been Jinny's home since she was three years old. She and Lesli had been the only survivors in an apartment building fire in Vancouver when both parents had been lost.

'Does your grandfather still believe there's a pot of gold on the property?' Bret asked.

'How do you know there isn't?' she challenged, bristling.

'We found enough in the stream alone last year to have the barn re-roofed!'

His head shook in disbelief. 'Jinny, don't tell me he's got *you* believing that old tale now! It's a pipe-dream—an old man's pipe-dream.'

'Maybe so,' she said stubbornly, breathing hard through her nostrils so that they flared whitely. 'But I'll thank you to keep your opinions to yourself when you see him. He's an old man now, and he's had little enough to dream about in his lifetime. He took on the job of raising Lesli and me, though goodness knows it must have been the last thing he wanted right then. Grandmother had just died, and he was a man alone away out here, but he took us in and cared for us.'

The amusement had gone from Bret's eyes when he looked at her again, and his voice sounded odd in its gentleness, as if he had had little cause to use that quality for a long time. 'Okay, Jinny. I won't say anything to spoil his dream.'

Denis O'Brien still sat in his favourite wing-backed chair where Jinny had left him. The log fire had burnt away to ashen embers while he dozed over a book on his lap, his steel-rimmed glasses perched on the end of his sharply pointed nose.

'Is that you, Jinny?' he asked querulously as he stirred from sleep.

'Yes, it's me, Pop, and I've brought a visitor for you. You remember Bret, don't you? Bret Stafford?'

'Bret? Oh, I thought it was that policeman fellow you were bringing back with you. How are you, Bret? Sure, it's good to see your face again after so long. What brings you back to the Valley?'

'Pop!' Jinny said, exasperated, kneeling before the fireplace to coax reluctant flames from the white ash. 'Bret came back for the funeral.'

'Funeral? Oh, yes—Henry died, didn't he? I'm sorry,

boy, that it's a sad occasion that brings you back.'

'That's all right, Mr O'Brien,' Bret said, shaking the frail hand Denis held out to him and pulling up a hard-backed chair to sit close to the old man. 'I hadn't seen my father for—a long time.'

'No, I suppose that's true. Let's see now, didn't you leave about the same time as Lesli? But it wasn't you she married, was it?'

'I'll make some of your special tea, Pop,' said Jinny, rising abruptly from the hearth. Most of the time her grandfather's mind was clear, but occasionally, as now, people and events became confused.

'Good idea, Jinny. Make some for Bret, too.' Denis turned his white head to Bret and winked one of the piercing blue eyes that had lost none of their colour over the years. 'Jinny makes a grand cup of tea.'

Jinny took off her jacket and hat and busied herself in the small kitchen across the hall, hearing only a murmur of voices from the living room as she laced her grandfather's tea liberally with the brandy he loved. She hesitated over Bret's cup, then shrugged and dosed his tea the same way. Somehow, she suspected that brandy would appeal to him more than straight tea.

After arranging some of the cookies she had baked the day before on a plate, she carried the tray across the hall and her heart skipped a beat when she heard her grandfather's voice.

'So now you'll be running Valley Ranch, Bret! I'm surprised your father had enough sense to leave the place to you.'

'It's as much of a surprise to me as it is to you, Mr O'Brien,' Bret said quietly, 'but I won't be running it. I've had a good offer already from the Sunrise Cattle Company, and——' He broke off sharply as Jinny clashed the tray down on a table close by and turned to face him, her cheeks a furious red.

'A *cattle* company? You're thinking of selling to *them*?'

'They've made me a pretty good offer, Jinny, and——'

'A good offer?' she interrupted passionately. 'Don't you think your father could have accepted their offers over the past seven years? And why do you think he didn't? Because he wanted his son, and his son's sons, to carry on the Stafford name in Gold Valley!'

Bret's skin had paled and his eyes were slate grey as he pushed back his chair and stood up. 'If my father had wanted me to carry on the name, he'd have treated me as his son long ago. No, Jinny,' he said bitterly, 'there won't be any sons from me to carry on the Stafford name.'

'Come along now, my boy,' said Denis in a placating tone. 'Sit down again and enjoy your tea. Don't pay any attention to Jinny—she has a tongue as sharp as her grandmother's, and that's saying something, I can tell you. Bring the tea, Jinny, and I hope it's cooler than your temper!' The old man glared at her from under bushy white eyebrows, and she brought his and Bret's teacups to the side table between them. Bret had resumed his seat, but his brow was set in an angry frown.

'I'm sorry, Bret,' she got out with difficulty. 'It's not my business whether or not you let strangers take over the ranch.'

He expelled his breath in a long-drawn sigh as he looked at her prettily flushed face framed by curling tendrils of black hair. 'I'm doing very well with my charter plane business,' he explained in a slow voice he might have used to a rebellious child, 'and I can do even better with the capital I'd get from the sale of the ranch. Anyway,' he threw a dismissing hand into the air, 'it's been seven years since I've been near a horse or a cow—what do I know of ranching now?'

'That's a poor excuse, Bret Stafford, and you know it!' Jinny flashed back. 'You loved the ranch once, and the mountains, and the Valley.' Scorn crept into her final words. 'Any man who can build a charter plane business from nothing shouldn't find it too difficult to take over a well-run ranch!'

Denis, who had been sipping his tea appreciatively while looking from one to the other of them, now put in sharply: 'That's enough now, Jinny! Let Bret drink his tea and tell me about this business of his.'

For another moment Bret glared into Jinny's eyes, then turned away to take up the cup and swallow half its contents in one gulp. Jinny watched, fascinated, while his expression changed to one of shock as a bout of coughing left his face red.

'My God,' he choked out at last, 'did he say—this is tea?'

Denis chuckled. 'Jinny knows how to warm the cockles of a man's heart with her tea.'

'She could also choke a man to death with it!' Bret returned wryly, his voice still distorted.

'I'd have thought brandy was more in your line than tea,' Jinny remarked with deceptive mildness.

'Maybe so. But normally when I drink brandy I know what to expect, and the same with tea.' He looked unsmilingly at her. 'Now that I know what to expect, may I have another cup?'

'That's the boy,' Denis said delightedly, turning to Jinny. 'I'll have another myself, darlin'.'

'You're not supposed to——'

'Oh, just one more won't harm me,' he wheedled. 'To celebrate Bret's homecoming.'

'Very well. It can be your farewell drink to him at the same time,' Jinny told him tartly, and saw Bret's head swivel sharply towards her.

'I have to see to the horses,' she announced loftily when she came back from the kitchen with their replenished cups, and went to her bedroom to change into warm brown slacks and a heavy-knit sweater.

The snow had stopped, and a pale late afternoon sun slanted from behind the mountains across the wide valley as she crossed to the stables. She paused for a moment to lean on the fence separating them from the house area and wondered how Bret could think of leaving the splendour of this Valley to the impersonal efficiency of a cattle company. His younger voice still echoed in her mind from one of the many occasions when Lesli had prodded him about leaving the Valley for the excitement beyond the mountains. 'This is the most beautiful spot in the world,' he had said fervently, 'and I'll never leave it.' Yet he *had* left it not long after, when Lesli went off with Eddie Clark in search of the adventures she craved.

Careen and Fitz, the mare and stallion the O'Brien ranch boasted, welcomed her arrival in the stables with gentle blowings through their nostrils and an anxious-eyed following of her movements to the oats barrel. Jinny exclaimed in annoyance when she remembered that fresh hay would have to be brought down from the store loft above. She went up the wooden ladder, leaving the horses happily munching their ration of oats, and muttered under her breath about the short-sightedness of the men who had stacked the hay too tightly under the roof. Her stomach muscles knotted tightly as she reached upwards to poke with little result at the close-packed hay, and gasped when she felt the pitchfork being taken roughly from her hands.

'Don't you have any help around here?' Bret said angrily from behind her. 'This isn't work for a girl!'

'Tommy Stiles comes in after school and on Saturdays,' Jinny told him breathlessly. 'And we have help with the haying ...'

She looked on while Bret threw his jacket on the rail and exercised powerful muscles on the recalcitrant pile, tossing the fork quickly over the side until a sizeable amount lay below them.

His breath had scarcely altered its pace when he put

down the pitchfork at last, and she realised how fit he had
kept himself in spite of the city life he led. The taut ripple
of shoulder muscles was evident even in the simple act of
replacing his jacket, and Jinny thought involuntarily how
attractive he must be to the women who supplied all his
needs except marriage. She looked at the clear-cut shape of
his mouth, its sensuous lines almost obliterated by the firmness with which he held it as he turned to her. What would
it be like to be kissed by him? He must be very practised by
now.

'How many cows are you running?' he asked tersely.

'Only—about seventy-five,' she stammered, startled by
the turn her thoughts had taken.

'That's far too many for you to handle yourself,' he
snapped. 'Why doesn't your grandfather sell the place and
move into town?'

'Because this is Pop's home!' She took a step closer to
him and looked up into his face with flushed cheeks. 'He's
lived here for more than fifty years ... he wouldn't know
what to do with himself anywhere else. Besides'—her voice
dropped to a lower key—'he wouldn't want any cattle company to reap the benefits of the——' She stopped suddenly
when his hands shot out to grip her shoulders, and she felt
the lean hardness of his fingers as he shook her and looked
with stormy grey eyes into hers.

'Reap the benefit of the *gold*?' he finished for her, his lip
curling with scorn. 'Can't you get it into your head, Jinny,
that—there—is—no—gold—on—this—property?'   He
shook her emphatically between each word, and her eyes
were a shocked lilac as they looked up into his. He glared at
her in silence for another moment before his eyes went
dazedly to his hands on her shoulders, then he dropped
them.

'Your grandfather's a dreamer, Jinny, and I know there's
no way he'll give up his dream of gold now after all these
years, but *you*——' He shook his head and gestured round

the barn. 'Keeping this place going for the sake of an old man's dream is nothing short of craziness!'

'I manage very well,' she said shortly, and moved to the ladder to go with light steps down it, turning to face him with hands on her hips when **he** came to join her. 'We've heard of Women's Lib even out here in Gold Valley, you know! I can do anything a man can do—and do it better most of the time.'

'Like pulling that hay out up there?' he asked with a sarcastic flick of his head to the loft.

'I'd have managed. I've lived very well without your help for the past seven years, Bret Stafford!'

He looked at her in brooding silence for several seconds, then asked mockingly: 'And what does your policeman friend think of your liberated ideas? He seemed a pretty chauvinistic type to me.'

Jinny's colour rose, and her eyes dropped from his. 'Mike —doesn't come out here often. Pop doesn't care for men who wear a uniform.'

'That must make the romance difficult.'

Jinny opened her mouth to deny a romance, then remembered Bret's obliging string of women in Vancouver and changed it to a brief: 'We get by.'

'Mmm. Well,' he turned and went to the open doorway, 'I should get back and talk to Frank Milner. He'll have more to do with the sale than I'll have time for.'

'Bret?' His head came round to look enquiringly at her, and she added softly: 'Do you really have to sell the ranch?'

His shoulders lifted in a semi-shrug. 'I haven't much choice, Jinny. I can't split myself in two, and—this place hasn't too many happy memories for me.' He lifted a hand in a gesture of farewell and stepped across the slushy enclosure in shoes that were more suitable to the boardroom than the stockyard.

Something about the set of his well-toned shoulders

brought a flood of memories to Jinny's mind, visions of the younger Bret in denim shirt and jeans, or the best suit Lesli had insisted on if he escorted her further than the local drug store's soda fountain.

Probably the expertly cut suit he wore now was one of many such in his wardrobe, but Jinny knew with the sharpness of the cold air she drew into her lungs that the Bret underneath them was still the man she had dreamed of for so many years. Yet he was further away from her now, in his life style and outlook, than he had been when she was a girl of fourteen.

CHAPTER TWO

'YOU'RE very quiet tonight,' Mike Preston remarked the following Saturday evening as they drove away from the O'Briens' Hillside Ranch. It had become a habit for him to call for Jinny and take her to the only regularly scheduled entertainment in Gold Valley, a dance held in the Community Centre every week. The dances were always well attended, not only by the young people of the area, but by the more established members of the community.

'Am I?' Jinny asked indifferently, the flatness in her voice reflecting the sense of letdown she felt at not having seen Bret again before he left. That he would have gone from the Valley by now she was sure. There would be nothing to hold him there once he had put the sale of Valley Ranch into motion. She hadn't expected that he would feel any obligation to say goodbye to her, but her grandfather was another matter. Bret had said he was closer to the old man than he had been to his father, but evidently that hadn't meant he felt a farewell visit was necessary.

'I'll check your coat, Jinny,' Mike said when they were

inside the square red brick building, and took the white cloth coat she had worn over a dress of deep purple, a colour that emphasised the deep blue of her eyes. While she waited for Mike's return from the cloakroom her eyes roved over the couples dancing in the largest room the Centre boasted. Nearly all were familiar to her, including the six-man band which managed to produce a variety of music to suit differing tastes.

Her heart missed a beat, then raced dizzily when she recognised Bret's distinctive figure dancing with Carol Holmes, whose blonde good looks were popular with males of all ages for miles around. He hadn't left Gold Valley!

The knowledge sang in her veins as Mike led her to the long corner table where they normally gathered with their friends. Most of them were dancing now, but Sandra and Bob, a couple recently engaged, made room at the table for Jinny and Mike.

'Who's the man Carol's dancing with?' Sandra asked a few minutes later. 'Trust her to latch on to the dreamiest man in town.'

'Hey!' Bob protested. 'I'm supposed to be the dreamiest man in town as far as you're concerned.'

'So you are, honey,' she soothed him with a dazzling smile. 'I meant the dreamiest *stranger* in town.'

'He isn't a stranger,' Jinny put in quietly. 'He's Bret Stafford, from Valley Ranch.'

'Virtually a stranger, though, Jinny,' Mike corrected, giving her a swift look from under his brows. 'As I hear it, he's been away from Gold Valley for years.'

Before she could make a reply, the others returned from the dance floor and in the flurry of greetings the subject of Bret Stafford was dropped. But Jinny noticed, with an un-reasonable pang of dismay, that Bret had returned with Carol to her table and taken the seat beside her.

Later, dancing in Mike's stalwart arms, her eyes met the cool grey of Bret's over Carol's blonde head and she forced a smile of recognition to her lips. Two dances later, Bret came to stand beside her and ask her to dance, a request that brought Mike's brows down in a quick frown as he glanced up at Bret's smoothly handsome profile.

Jinny nodded, forgetting Mike's obvious displeasure the instant Bret's arms closed round her and they began to move in time to the music. He held her so close that she could detect the faint odour of expensive cologne on his face, feel the lean hardness of his body against hers, the sinewy strength of his arm encircling her waist. She pulled away slightly to look up into his face.

'I—I thought you'd have gone by now,' she said breathlessly.

His eyes were shadowed in the half-light of the dance floor as he looked down at her; perhaps, she thought, that was why they seemed to reflect a greenish cast.

'No, Jinny,' he said at last, a whimsical smile softening the firm line of his mouth. 'I did a lot of thinking when I got home the other day, and I decided to try splitting myself in two—for a while, anyway.'

'Did you, Bret?' Her violet eyes shone upwards with a melting sheen that brought a tightening of his hand on hers. 'I'm glad you decided to do the right thing, after all.'

'What makes you so sure it's the right thing?' he asked, suddenly gruff. 'I could mess the whole operation up! I'm more at home in a cockpit than a saddle these days.' His arm drew her closer again and he spoke into her ear, growing eagerness lifting his voice from its deeper pitch. 'But I can combine both as far as the ranch goes. I'm planning on clearing off a landing strip close to the house and having a plane up here so that I can keep an eye on cattle movement from above. It would be a fantastic improvement on spending days on a horse going nowhere fast.'

The music stopped, but he made no attempt to release her or take her back to her table. Instead, he went on talking.

'Ranching's into the space age now, Jinny. In a plane, I can cover as much territory in a day as would take a week or more on horseback. And in ranching, like any other business, time is money.'

His feet moved again when the music began, and her own followed dreamily. She knew he needed no comment from her. The vibrancy of his enthusiasm was an almost tangible thing between them, and she was content to be his silent audience for these few precious minutes.

'Excuse me,' Mike's controlled voice came from beside them. 'I think this is my dance, Jinny.'

Before Jinny could protest, Bret had apologised to Mike and disappeared between the other dancers. She looked furiously into Mike's impassive face as he replaced Bret's arms with his own and moved forward.

'Why did you do that, Mike? You know we hadn't planned on dancing this one together.'

'He asked for one dance, not the entire evening,' Mike returned bluntly. 'You came with me, and I'm not about to be made of fool of by Bret Stafford or anyone else. Do you think I enjoy sitting twiddling my thumbs at the table while he whispers in your ear?'

Jinny's colour rose to angry redness, but she bit back the sharp words that came to her lips. Although she hated the belligerently possessive note in Mike's voice, he was right in as much as that she had come to the dance with him. Their friends looked on them as a couple, and she could understand the hurt to his pride when she had not returned after the first dance with Bret.

'Bret was just telling me of his plans for Valley Ranch,' she said with forced restraint. 'He's decided not to sell right now.'

'Oh?' The news that Bret would be staying in the area seemed to give Mike little pleasure. 'I'd like to bet that's not what he's whispering in Carol's ear at this minute!'

Jinny's head turned sharply, bringing it into a direct line

of vision with Bret, whose head was bent close to Carol's pink ear saying something that brought a delightedly shocked smile to the girl's face.

The rest of the evening went by for Jinny in an agony of slowness while she did her best to ignore the fact that Bret had spent most of it in Carol's company. But at last the time came when she felt she could reasonably ask Mike to take her home without rousing comment from the other members of the group, but Mike gave her a concerned glance as they walked to his car.

'What's wrong with you tonight, Jinny? You've been acting strange ever since I called for you. It hasn't anything to do with Stafford, has it?'

'Why would I be concerned with Bret Stafford?' she countered sharply. 'It was my sister he went out with, not me. The type of man he's become doesn't appeal to me in the slightest.'

'I'm glad to hear that, Jinny,' Mike said quietly, pausing before unlocking the car door. 'I've seen his kind of smooth operator before, and girls always end up getting hurt by them.'

'Not this girl!'

Jinny sounded positive at the car, but later when she lay sleepless in bed the untruth of her words came back to haunt her. The dream that had lain dormant for seven long years had awakened to a demanding longing as unfamiliar to her as she was powerless to overcome it. Perhaps it was her fate that, as Mike had predicted, she would be hurt in the end, but she knew with unfailing certainty that it was a risk she had no choice but to take.

It was two days later when Jinny learned that Bret had returned to the city. She was checking the cows due to calve that spring in the verdant green of the meadows lying alongside the lake. Only an occasional patch of snow still remained to dot the meadows which reached up to the nearby mountains, where the lower slopes were clad in the darker green of spreading pines before reaching the craggy rock face and ultimate topping of glistening snow.

Jinny pulled the mare, Careen, to a halt and her eyes searched the distant crags for signs of Endor, the eagle who returned with his mate every year about this time to take possession of the nest they had built years before far up the cliffside. Jinny had named him 'Endor' from a scarcely re-membered mythical tale because it seemed to suit the cool remoteness of his majestic sweeps across the Valley in search of prey to feed his youngsters.

It was only during the past two summers that Endor had, seemingly, accepted Jinny as part of the surrounding land-scape and he would come to alight on a tree near her, the warm yellow of his eyes belying the stern curve of beak that was merciless with lake fish and small rodents around the property.

Endor hadn't returned yet, she decided, and headed Careen back to the ranch. They were rounding the corner of the bush-edged lake when a voice called from the Stafford land a few yards away.

'Hey, Jinny! How are things?'

Jinny cantered over to where Frank Milner, the manager of Valley Ranch, sat on a magnificent bay gelding. She liked Frank. Although he was unmarried, he had the re-liable maturity of a father for Jinny. He was fast approach-ing middle age, his dark hair winged with white, and she wondered again why he had never taken a wife. He was good-looking now with his lean weather-tanned features, and must have been devastating when he was younger.

'Hi, Frank,' she called as she approached. 'Everything's fine with me. How about you? I guess you're glad the ranch isn't going to be sold after all?'

He gave her a slow smile. 'I sure am, Jinny. The cattle company man told me I'd get the job of managing it for them just the same, but it suits me better to work for a

Stafford. When Bret gets back, we——'

'Bret's gone?' she asked quickly.

'Just to get his plane business tidied away. He won't be doing any of the flying himself, of course, now he's taken on the ranch as well. He'll just be kind of a figurehead for the air company.' Frank looked contemplatively at his saddle horn. 'He'll be a lot different to work for than his dad was. He's keen enough, but all these new ideas he has for the ranch—well, I don't know how they'll work out.' He shook his head as if mystified, and Jinny came quickly to Bret's defence.

'It's a different world now, Frank, from when these ranches were begun. I think Bret has some very good ideas, and a more modern way of looking at things that can make him a success as a rancher as well as a businessman.'

'You're probably right, Jinny—as long as he doesn't fall between two stools. Flying and ranching are a long way apart.' Frank gave her a sidelong glance that took in the fervour of her dark blue eyes, the healthy pink of her cheeks, the curling length of her black hair under a short-brimmed white hat. 'He'd do better with a wife to help him.'

'I don't believe Bret finds a wife necessary in his scheme of things,' she replied stiffly, and turned Careen's head back towards home. 'Excuse me, Frank, I have to get back to see to my grandfather now.'

'Bret had that Carol Holmes out to the ranch on Sunday,' he called after her. 'It would be a shame if he settled on the likes of her for a wife, wouldn't it?'

Jinny reined Careen in and looked back at the manager. 'He brought Carol out to the ranch?' She herself had never entered the Stafford house, and the thought of Carol having been there sent a stab of jealousy through her.

'He did,' Frank confirmed solemnly. 'Said she wanted to see round the place, but they didn't budge far from the house.'

'Well, that's his business, isn't it, Frank?' she said after a moment's tremulous thought. 'I really have to go—see you around.' She put a heel to Careen, scarcely seeing Frank's wave of farewell or the pensive smile on his face. Her thoughts kept a rhythm with the pound of Careen's hooves on the soggy turf they traversed. That Bret had spent an evening at a dance in Carol's company was one thing. That he had taken her to his home put an entirely different complexion on it.

Days passed in a round of routine chores for Jinny until a week after her meeting with Frank. That day, Endor returned. As if seeking to renew her acquaintance after a long winter spent abroad, the white-headed bald eagle circled close to where she worked with the newborn calves, settling at last on the uppermost branch of an aspen whose branches showed only the barest promise of bursting leaf to come.

'Pop!' she explained loudly on entering the house a short time later. 'Endor's back! He came and——'

She pulled up abruptly in the doorway of the small living room when a denim-clad figure rose from beside her grandfather. Bret, familiar yet strange in the newness of his work clothes, stood up and looked at her, one dark eyebrow winging up to an interrogative point.

'Who's back?' Denis asked testily from his chair. 'Oh, it's that eagle you're talking about.' To Bret he said in a half amused, half ashamed voice: 'My grandchild thinks she has made friends with a creature of the wilds.'

'He *is* my friend,' Jinny threw in hotly, coming into the room and taking off her jacket. 'Every year he comes back to this spot and lets me know he's here.'

'It's a wonder he hasn't been winged by hunters long before now,' Bret remarked mildly, resuming his seat.

'Endor stays away from the hunters,' she told him loftily. 'He's a lot wiser than most people, let alone birds.'

'All right, darlin',' Denis soothed. 'Though I think you'd

be better off if you knew more about people than the wild creatures. Why don't you make us some tea now you're home?'

'Not for me, thanks,' said Bret, getting to his feet and seeming taller in the short denim jacket. 'We'll have that game of chess real soon, Mr O'Brien.'

'That we will, Bret. I'll look forward to it, so don't be too long in coming back.'

Jinny followed Bret's tall figure to the door.

'Are you sure Carol won't mind your spending time playing chess with Pop?' she asked sweetly.

He turned back from the porch steps and grimaced. 'I'd forgotten how fast news travels in these parts.' He looked levelly into her eyes. 'Carol—or any other woman—has no say in how I spend my time. I'll be around to play chess with your grandfather.'

He left then and, true to his word, turned up the very next evening after supper for the promised game. Jinny felt a surge of pleasure each time she looked up from the embroidery she was working on by the fire. It was wonderful to her to see the rapt concentration on her grandfather's face, the closely knit brow of Bret as they pored over the ivory chess men.

It became a habit for Bret to drop by several evenings a week, occasions her grandfather looked forward to keenly. As it was impossible for Denis to keep quiet about the subject that had been close to his heart for so many years— Hillside gold—Jinny felt grateful to Bret for his seeming acceptance of the old man's fantasy. At times, she could almost believe that his interest in the mythical seam was genuine.

He never came at weekends, and Jinny presumed they were reserved for Carol. She herself went twice more to the Community Centre dance with Mike, and on the second occasion the pain of seeing Bret's dark head close to Carol's all evening was almost more than she could bear. Although he didn't ask her to dance again, Jinny realised that she was being unfair to Mike.

She tried to be as tactful as possible when they sat in Mike's car outside Hillside later that evening, but his face was set in grim lines when she told him she wouldn't be able to see much of him in future. 'Pop needs me more and more,' she said in a low voice, feeling hypocritical when he looked disbelievingly at her in the slanting light of a silvery moon.

'For heaven's sake, Jinny,' he burst out, 'you're young! You can't spend the rest of his life babysitting an old man!' His tone changed then to one of reluctant concern. 'Is he sicker now than he was before?'

'No,' she admitted honestly. 'Since Bret's been coming to play chess with him, he seems to have improved slightly.'

'Stafford's been coming to the house?' he asked suspiciously. 'You're sure he's not the reason for not wanting to come out with me?'

'What makes you think that?' she asked, turning away to hide the hurt in her eyes. 'It's Pop's company he enjoys, not mine.'

'And Carol's,' he added drily, putting out a hand to gently move her face back towards his. 'You know I want to marry you, Jinny. Does this mean you'll never want to, or are you really just worried about your grandfather?'

'Oh, Mike!' she said miserably, and felt the sudden warm assurance of his mouth on hers in a tender kiss. For a few moments she gave herself up to the safe familiarity of it, but when his lips sought to deepen the pressure she pulled away as if in panic. However useless her dreams were, Bret's were the arms she wanted round her, Bret's the lips to demand her surrender to masculine control. 'I'm sorry, Mike,' she whispered.

'I guess that gives me the answer to my question,' he said bitterly. 'It's Bret Stafford, isn't it?'

She hesitated, her eyes large as they met his, then nodded numbly.

'I think you're in for a heap of trouble,' Mike told her grimly. 'But I hope for your sake he turns out to be worth it.'

Jinny stumbled from the car without another word and watched as Mike reversed noisily and shot away from the house at top speed. Tears blinded her eyes as she staggered blindly up the porch steps. If only she could have loved Mike! With him, she would have known nothing but loyalty and devotion, qualities most women would be grateful for in a husband, whereas with Bret ... even if he could bring himself to the point of marriage, his wife would surely never feel security in his affection.

Like Endor, the eagle who allowed her to come just so close while holding her at a distance, Bret would always have to be free to soar to the remote fastness of his private domain. The only difference between them was that Bret's wings were man-made and therefore vulnerable, as Endor's could never be.

The building of the airstrip was accomplished with such remarkable speed that Jinny was surprised to hear, two weeks later when she was skirting the lake on Fitz, the sudden reverberations of an engine echoing from one mountain to another and sending the cattle stampeding in every direction.

Shielding her eyes from the sun, she looked for and found the small white plane with red markings which was already a blurred dot down the Valley. Some of Bret's enthusiasm as he told her grandfather about his planned airstrip had rubbed off on her, but now, with her cows running amok and even Endor squawking in his rough voice as he veered off into the mountains, she felt only frustration. How could Bret, who surely hadn't forgotten how easily

cows could be spooked by strange noises, be so uncaring of
the new mothers in the O'Brien herd?

With sinking heart, she saw that the youngest calf, running in panic to the protection of his mother, had cata-
pulted himself into the lake and was now uttering piercing
cries as he sank deeper into the mud with every frantic
effort he made to loose himself. Jinny shook her fist im-
potently at the disappearing speck of Bret's plane and got
down from Fitz, who was also snickering nervously.

Taking the rope that hung from her saddle, she approached the mired calf slowly, one part of her mind sending up a prayer of thanks that it was not one of the larger
animals trapped there, though the mother cow, crazed with
fear for her bawling offspring, was bellowing her en-
couragement and threatening to plunge into the mud after
him.

Jinny quickly made a noose at the end of the rope and
flung it out towards the calf, relieved when it caught round
his neck on the third try. Gradually, and to the accompani-
ment of noisily outraged maternal sensibilities, the calf was
drawn inexorably out of the mud to shore.

Sweat beaded Jinny's brow as the young animal came
closer and she shrugged off the jacket she wore, keeping one
hand on the rope to hold it steady. A restless whinny from
Fitz alerted her to the return of Bret's plane, and she saw
with dismay the quick, frightened jerk of the horse's head
against the loosely tied reins as he freed himself and
galloped instantly off in the direction of home. Then, as the
noise of the plane's engine grew to deafening proportions,
the mother cow gave a final bellow and deserted her calf for
the safety of overhanging trees some distance away.

Jinny hung on grimly to the rope while the calf reared in
terror and fell back into the mud, dragging her with him
until she was mired to the top of her jeans. The plane
dipped lower, then winged away towards the Stafford ranch

while Jinny, immobile in the oozing mud, shook her fist and raged at it.

Fear came to her seconds later when she realised that her legs were stuck fast in the thick brown slime. The calf's frantic struggles only served to pull them deeper into it, and now the mother returned to bellow ferociously at the water's edge. Tears of angry self-pity edged from Jinny's eyes when she visualised her grandfather's reaction to the news that she had suffocated in the mud of his own lake. It would be enough to bring on his own final heart attack! Minutes passed while she wallowed in the drama of the imagined scene, so absorbed that she failed to hear the lesser sound of a four-wheel-drive vehicle pull up close by.

Bret suddenly appeared from behind the bushy thicket, his look of hurried concern giving way to cynical amusement as a torrent of abuse flew from Jinny's lips.

'You and your damn plane!' she threw up at him, unaware of the comical picture she presented. 'Look what you've done! You've not only damaged one of our best calves, you've almost killed *me*!'

He waited until she ran out of breath, then took a step towards her in leather boots that reached almost to his knees. Dark watery mud enveloped the highly polished brown and seeped upwards over the soft leather at his instep.

'Your grandfather's right,' he remarked mildly, pausing to look down at her with a half smile. 'You have a sharp tongue. Maybe you'll believe me now when I say a girl like you is biting off more than she can chew in taking on a place this size.'

Jinny stared at him in speechless rage for a moment, forgetting the indignity of her position, then said through clenched teeth: 'Get me out of this mud before it reaches my ears.'

One dark eyebrow rose with infuriating slowness. 'Would

it hurt to say "please"?—or is that against your liberated principles?'

He cut short her angry splutterings by bending down to reach under her arms, pulling her up with a steady motion until she left the clinging mud with a sickening sucking noise, her jeans and red and white checked shirt turned to an éven dun colour. For a fractional moment he held her to him, and she felt the reassuring hardness of his body against hers before he lifted her on to dry ground behind them. It gave her a savage sense of satisfaction to see that dark smudges had been transferred to his shirt and jeans from hers.

He said nothing, but turned back to catch the rope she had dropped when he lifted her, and within a very short time calf was reunited with his mother, who set to with loud strokes of her moist tongue to clean the mud from him.

'You'd better come back to the house with me,' said Bret, eyeing Jinny distastefully. 'I can't deliver you back to your grandfather looking like that.'

'And whose fault is it that I look like this?' she demanded angrily.

'Obviously you think it's mine. I'd have thought the animals would be used to planes by now. Don't any fly over this way?'

'*Over*,' she gritted through her teeth, which were beginning to chatter with cold. 'Not *beside*!'

He shrugged and picked up her jacket and a blanket he had come prepared with, draping it round her shoulders and urging her with his arm towards the Land Rover. The rough fibres of the blanket felt abrasively warm against her neck, and she tried not to let the mud clinging wetly to her clothes smear the passenger seat as he helped her in.

Hunched in miserable silence, she was scarcely aware of the rough terrain under the wheels as Bret drove bumpily to the ranch and came round at last to lift her down to the gravelled forecourt in front of the house.

'Come on,' he said gruffly, holding her away slightly. 'Mrs Trent will see to the washing and drying of your clothes.'

Jinny shrank back into the blanket as if she was coming out of a dream. The tall and gaunt Stafford housekeeper had been a familiar figure to her for years, but Olive Trent had always made it clear that she shared old Henry Stafford's antipathy towards the O'Briens.

'No! Take me home, Bret, I can wash my clothes myself.'

'Nonsense,' he said briskly. 'You say it's my fault you're in this state, so it's the least I can do. Besides, the shock of seeing you like this could give your grandfather another attack.'

She glanced up into his unrevealing face, wondering if his concern for her grandfather could be genuine, but before she could come to a decision his arm was propelling her firmly towards the pillared porch and into the house she had never before entered. Curiosity overcame diffidence, and her eyes went round the low-ceilinged hall with its polished wood floor and carefully tended furniture.

To her left lay a spacious living room with a massive rock fireplace dominating one wall, and fanning off from the rear of the hall were passages that presumably led to the kitchen and bedroom quarters. Bret urged her down one of the passages and stopped to open the second door on their left.

'You can use this room,' he said, ushering her into a twin-bedded room which was obviously unoccupied by anyone in the house. Jinny felt an odd sense of relief that it wasn't his own room Bret had taken her to.

'There's a bathroom attached,' he went on, 'and lots of hot water. Leave your things outside, and I'll have Mrs Trent see to them.' He went to the door and turned back to add: 'Come into the living room when you're ready and I'll have a drink waiting for you.'

Left alone, Jinny looked round the meticulously tidy room and into the adjoining bathroom where sunshine yellow towels adorned the rails as if there was nothing unusual in having unexpected guests desiring hot baths at Valley Ranch. The mud had begun to dry and harden on the front of her shirt and jeans, and suddenly nothing could have looked more inviting to her than the wide, pale primrose bathtub that conjured up visions of hot steamy water enveloping her. Quickly she stripped off the dirt-caked clothes and dropped them, together with the blanket, outside the door with a guilty feeling of imposing on the Stafford housekeeper—an imposition she was sure would not be appreciated.

Scented bath oil beads sent a heather fragrance curling round her hair as she lay supine much longer than she should have, and when she did at last step from the bath to wrap herself in the thickness of a bath towel, her skin glowed a warm pink. She rubbed herself dry, then wrapped a clean towel about her, wondering if Bret expected her to appear like that in the living room for the promised drink. But she saw when she re-entered the bedroom that a dark red silk-like robe had been left on one of the beds. Presumably it had been left there by Mrs Trent, although the owner was obviously a man. Bret?

The dark folds of the robe fell in a crumpled heap round her feet even when she had tied it tightly at the waist, and the sleeves had to be turned back several times before her hands were visible. Surveying herself in the full-length mirror on the closet door, she made an instant decision to wait there until the housekeeper brought back her clothes. Nothing would induce her to show herself to Bret Stafford, the connoisseur of women, in this garb. Her hair, curling damply to her shoulders, had a wild, unkempt look which she was sure he would find unattractive in any of the women he knew.

'Jinny? Are you presentable?'

Bret's tap at the door and normal-sounding voice sent a quiver of apprehension through her and made her: 'No!—no, I'm not!' sound strangled even to herself.

His voice came through the panel again, this time with an impatient tinge. 'Well, hurry up. I've poured a drink for you and lit the fire in the living room.'

'I—I'll be there in a minute,' she called back weakly, and spent a minute or two trying to improve her appearance by tightening the belt still further and smoothing her hands over her springing hair several times. Then, with a last despairing glance in the mirror, she opened the door cautiously and went on bare feet along the carpeted passage, acutely conscious of her nakedness under the silky red robe.

Bret, wearing a thick white sweater and clean denim trousers, stood at one of the wide living room windows looking moodily out to the forecourt, and Jinny took advantage of his abstraction by glancing round the square-shaped room, where again the furniture was cold but well cared for. There was a cold, unlived-in air about it in spite of the reflected glow of leaping flames from the huge fireplace lighting on the polished wood surfaces. She shivered, and one hand went up as if to hold the opening of the robe more closely together. The movement attracted Bret's attention and he swung round, his brow losing its frown as he took in her waif-like appearance. His eyes gave her a lingering scrutiny before he moved forward to take her by the hand and lead her to a corner of the sofa, which faced the blazing logs.

'I poured you a brandy,' he said, lifting his own glass as well as hers, handing hers to her before sitting down beside her. 'It's the only drink I'm sure you like.' One corner of his mouth quirked into a faint smile of irony as if he was recalling the special tea she had made for him and her grandfather.

Jinny looked at the deep glass almost filled with dark liquid and opened her lips to protest that she had never drunk brandy in her life, but the words died in her throat. The kind of woman Bret knew would never refuse a drink he had poured.

'Thank you,' she murmured with what she hoped was a sophisticated huskiness, and tipped the glass against the soft fullness of her lips, making a conscious effort not to choke as the spirit's fiery sting coursed its way down her throat. Her black lashes fanned the soft rosiness of her cheeks, hiding the sudden rush of tears to her eyes, and she felt the glass being taken gently from her fingers.

'You're supposed to sip it, Jinny,' Bret's voice, drily amused, came from beside her, and she raised eyes that had the dewy look of pansies to his face. 'Why didn't you tell me you don't drink?'

She got out a defiant: 'I do!' and he laughed.

'What? A glass of sherry at Christmas?'

Laughter softened the sarcasm in his voice, but Jinny's colour deepened. The women in his life had crystallised in her mind into one perfect woman. A poised, sophisticated blonde in command of every situation—the opposite of herself, in fact. Would he be sitting next to that vision of perfection with a tolerant smile of amusement as if she were a child? No, he would wait impatiently until she had finished her drink before taking her in his arms to kiss her passionately.

Passion was something Jinny knew about from reading more than from Mike's undemanding kisses, and always it had been Bret's face which had come between her and the more explicit passages in a book. She looked now at his clear-cut profile as it stared unseeingly into the flames, and the brandy, combined with the warmth from the fire, sent a lassitude she had never known before stealing through her body, and with it an upflowing urge to feel his firm lips on hers. Did the women he made love to make some sort of a sign of invitation before he took the initiative? Had Carol, here on this couch?

'Bret?'

'Mmm?'

He turned from his contemplation of the fire to look at her with vague enquiry, his arms remaining on his knees with both hands supporting the glass he held between them.

'Would—would you like to kiss me?'

'What?'

The startled lifting of his brows was unflattering in the extreme, and Jinny gulped miserably. She had forgotten for a moment her bedraggled appearance, one that Bret could never find attractive enough to even while away a few minutes of enforced idleness.

'I said——' she began faintly, but he interrupted her.

'Never mind,' he said hastily. 'I heard you.'

His eyes were suddenly alert as they searched her face. 'What's the idea, Jinny? Payment for services rendered? That's a big price to pay for the laundering of your clothes.'

'Of course it's not—payment,' she denied quickly. 'It was your fault I got into that mess, so there's no question of that. I just thought,' she straightened against the cushions and ran the pink tip of her tongue over her dry lower lip, 'that we could pass the time in a more—interesting way. But, of course, if you don't want to ...'

'I didn't say that,' he said in a slow voice that was only slightly touched with amusement. 'You really are liberated, aren't you?'

She watched in a trance while he put down his glass and turned to slide his arm across her shoulders, putting hard fingers under her chin to lift her mouth to the descent of his. Her eyes were wide as his lips touched hers and moved gently over their stiff contours. Paralysed, her senses were nonetheless acutely aware of the faint soap odour clinging to his skin, the sweep of dark hair away from his temple, the warmth of his breath against her cheek.

He lifted his head suddenly and looked closely at her with puzzled eyes. 'Doesn't that policeman of yours ever kiss you? Can't you relax a little?' His voice held a hint of impatience, and he added drily: 'And it helps if you close your eyes.'

She opened her lips to reply and his mouth swooped to cover them. Her mind reeled as his hand left her neck and slid across the smooth flesh of her shoulder under the robe before going down to hold the swelling firmness of her breast and move disturbingly there.

She moaned against his mouth and his head lifted again, his eyes holding the darkness of a stormy sea as they went quickly over her flushed cheeks and full mouth to the slender column of her throat and white skin beneath it where the silk robe had parted between her breasts. A shuddering sigh went through her when his lips found her there and travelled slowly up to the slight hollow in her throat where a pulse beat erratically, and with practised skill went along her cheekbone to claim her mouth again with savage pressure.

Her hands came up to push his head away, but instead they were suddenly at his nape, twining into the thickness of his hair and pressing his mouth closer. As if her action had released a spring in him, he moved his body to half cover hers, pressing her back against the cushions with such inexorable force that she panicked suddenly and pushed his face away with frenzied hands, sobbing: 'Bret—no!'

At once he sat up and away from her, his eyes heavy-lidded with emotion, his nostrils widened as his breath came raggedly through them. His eyes held the frightened awareness in hers for several seconds, then he gave a shaky laugh.

'For a liberated woman, you're very coy at the last minute!'

'Bret, I—I——' she stammered, her hand pulling together the robe over her nakedness as he rose to tower over her, her voice coming out in a squeal when he reached down suddenly and pulled her up against his obviously aroused body.

'A word of advice, Jinny,' he said tautly, grey eyes cold now. 'Don't offer what you can't deliver! You'll find most men won't be as——'

'The girl's clothes are ready,' a dry, disapproving voice said from the doorway, and Jinny gasped, turning in Bret's arms to see Olive Trent's tight-lipped look of censure. He, however, continued to hold her firmly, remotely cool when he addressed the housekeeper.

'Thanks, Mrs Trent. Put them in the bedroom.'

'Yours?' she asked with pointed sarcasm.

'In the one Miss O'Brien used for her bath.'

Mrs Trent sniffed at his formal use of Jinny's name, her narrow eyes giving the girl's figure a last insulting look before she turned and left.

Bret's arms dropped away when Jinny moved from him and she looked contritely into his hard set face, her nonchalance gone with the evaporation of the brandy's effects in her veins.

'I'm sorry, Bret,' she said in a low voice. 'It's my fault she thinks we——' She faltered to a stop and half turned away from his enigmatic gaze. 'The fact is, I'm not as liberated as you might think.'

'Really? You surprise me, Jinny!'

The sarcasm in his voice was lost on her, and she burst out: 'I hate somebody like her thinking I only came here to—to——'

'To what, Jinny?' he asked softly. 'Make love?' He came to stand in front of her and raise her chin with his fingers. 'Under the right circumstances, there's nothing more beautiful than making love—it's people like her who make something wrong of it.' He dropped her chin and turned away towards the fire muttering: 'She'd better get used to women around the place if she wants to stay here.'

Jinny blinked at his broad shoulders. 'You plan on getting married soon?' she asked constrictedly, and was disconcerted by his amused laugh as he looked back at her.

'Married? You really are a conventional little soul, aren't you? No, Jinny,' he shook his head, 'I've told you marriage isn't for me. Married woman always seem to want children, and that's not my scene at all. I don't feel it's at all necessary to perpetuate myself.'

She stared at him uncomprehendingly for a full minute after his head turned back to the flames. To her uncomplicated mind, he was as hard to understand as an alien from another planet. His physical needs, of which she had just been made startlingly aware, could be satisfied without the emotional ties of marriage and children—but wasn't that a sterile kind of way to live? Surely he needed the qualities a woman could supply apart from the obvious physical one? The intensity of her thoughts made her voice seem curt.

'This room at least could do with a wife's touch.'

'Oh?' He turned his back to the fire and looked at her with mild question. 'In what way could a wife improve it?'

'Well——' Trapped, Jinny looked round the room with appraising eyes. 'She could have the chairs and sofa recovered in bright florals instead of that dull brown velvet ... something light to contrast with the darkness of the wood, and ...' she moved across to the sombrely draped windows '... bright curtains to match. On this wide ledge she would have room for potted plants, and over there'— she pointed to the darkest corner of the room where bookshelves lined the wall—'she could have an arrangement of dried flowers and grasses. It's a beautiful house, Bret—you could have a homely room here where you could roast popcorn on the fire!' The last she added facetiously, and was surprised by the intent look he sent across to her.

'Were you ever in this house when my mother was alive?'

'No. I've never been in it until today.'

'Strange. You've just about described it the way it was before she died. Apart from the popcorn,' he added with a twisted smile. 'Dad wouldn't have allowed that.'

'Oh.' He seemed not to expect a reply, so she turned away. 'I—I guess I'd better get dressed. Pop will be wondering what happened to me.'

He looked back abstractedly into the fire, making no attempt to detain her and giving the impression that he had dismissed her from his mind.

If only she could send him out of hers as easily, she thought as she pulled on the freshly laundered clothes in the bedroom. But already hot waves of humiliation were sending prickly fingers over her skin. What had possessed her to make such a fool of herself, to think that a man of his sophistication wouldn't see through her thin defences to the naïve country girl underneath? How he must be laughing at her—if he was thinking of her at all!

As she slid her arms into her jacket and left the bedroom, she made an ardent vow that never again would she give him an opportunity to be amused by her inept amorous forays. She would be as coolly controlled as he was in their future encounters and perhaps, after a while, he would come to believe that the episode had meant no more to her than it had to him.

She sighed when she came out into the hall and saw his well-knit figure waiting for her by the front door. Would she ever come to believe that herself?

CHAPTER THREE

'WHERE'S Bret these days?' Denis O'Brien asked Jinny querulously ten days later. 'He never comes by for a game of chess now.'

'He went to the city, Pop,' she explained, a catch in her voice. 'He'll be coming along for a game any time now.'

She wished she herself could be as sure as her confident statement made her seem. It was true that Bret had left for Vancouver the day after she had been to Valley Ranch, but she knew that he had returned several days ago. Was he avoiding Hillside because of her? Because he didn't want the embarrassment—or boredom—of further scenes like the one that had taken place in his living room?

He needn't have worried, she thought resentfully, or punished her grandfather because of it. She had been schooling herself in the right attitude to adopt towards him ... friendliness tempered with coolness ... and as the days passed without seeing him, she felt her confidence grow.

It was two days later, when she had fed the horses earlier than usual, that she entered the house and saw him in his old position beside her grandfather's chair. The sight of his long body unwinding from his chair unnerved her, and all of her prepared attitudes crumbled when he looked with clear grey eyes into hers as if nothing had happened between them. Warm colour rushed to her cheeks as she glanced confusedly from one man to the other, and Denis's piercing blue eyes seemed to miss none of his grand-daughter's embarrassment as he looked shrewdly at her and then Bret.

'Bret's back from Vancouver, as you can see,' he said blandly. 'Why don't you make us some tea, darlin'?'

A gleam lit the coolness of Bret's eyes. 'I promise not to choke on it this time,' he said with mock gravity, and Jinny gave him a fleeting smile.

'How were things in the city?' she asked breathlessly.

He shrugged and sat down again. 'Same as always. The longer I stay here, the more I appreciate peace and quiet.'

Jinny's heart sang as she busied herself in the small kitchen preparing tea for the three of them. She'd always known that he loved the Valley with its lush pastures and soaring peaks which seemed to enclose everyone living there in a primitive tranquillity. She could never imagine that anyone who had known its peace and beauty would be satisfied with the hustle and bustle of city life.

In her mind she again compared Bret to Endor, the eagle who always seemed happy to come back to his accustomed nest in the Valley after wandering afar during the cold winter days. She put from her the thought that perhaps Endor greeted his warmer nest in the south with equal enthusiasm each autumn. Just as distasteful to her was the knowledge that Bret had in all likelihood seen at least one of the women in his life while he was in the city, and she pushed that thought away too. For the moment, she was content that he was here in her grandfather's house, bringing a touch of male companionship to the only other man she loved.

That she loved Bret, she now knew without doubt. Nights when she lay sleepless were filled with the wonder of a longing she had never known before that afternoon at Valley Ranch. She touched the places his lips had touched, wondering what he had felt when he had made love to her. He had been aroused, she knew, in the way a man could be desirous of a woman, but would he have been disappointed if she hadn't grown afraid suddenly and the normal fulfilment had taken place? Probably, she decided. Her inexperience in matters of love could only act as an irritant to a man used to expertly co-operative partners.

It became a habit for Bret to call in during the afternoons when Jinny was busy on the ranch, although he still spent an occasional evening playing chess or cribbage with Denis while she sat quietly by, reading or sewing. On the occasions when she came home earlier than usual, she would hear the deep murmur of their voices from the living room as she stood in the hall, and then an abrupt silence when they realised she was there.

'What do you and Bret talk about that's so secret?' she asked her grandfather one day, piqued that he should want to keep anything from her.

'Oh, this and that,' he answered vaguely. 'Man talk, you know.'

A sceptical look came into her eyes. 'What's so manly about it that I can't hear? I do a man's work on this ranch!'

As soon as the words left her lips, she wished she could snatch them back. Not for worlds would she hurt him by complaining of his inability to do ranch work any more.

'You won't always be doing a man's work, Jinny,' Denis said contritely, patting her shoulder as she knelt beside his chair. 'One day you'll have a husband and children to care for, as a woman should. Don't think it's been easy for me to see you do the work of two men about the place.'

'I know, Pop,' she cried, burying her face against his side, her voice coming in muffled half-tones. 'I didn't mean that I mind working the ranch—I just wish you could be the way you used to be. Riding out on Fitz to see to the cows, bringing in the hay, looking for gold in your spare time...'

As always, Denis's eyes brightened at the mention of gold. 'Bret's coming round to my way of thinking, I believe,' he said interestedly. 'He asks me a lot about where I think the seam lies, and so on. He's a fine lad—not like that old reprobate of a father he had!' His gnarled fingers lifted her chin from his side and he looked searchingly into her eyes. 'You like Bret well enough, don't you, child?'

She reached up to kiss his cheek, her eyes glistening with tears. 'Yes, Pop, I like him well enough,' she said gently.

Bret used his plane seldom, it seemed, and when he did he veered towards the further mountains on take-off, minimising the unsettling noise of the plane's engine. Whether because of this, or because the O'Brien cattle had become used to hearing it, few heads were raised from the green pasture when the familiar sound echoed across the Valley.

How dangerous this method of take-off was Jinny discovered when she accepted Bret's offer of a flight next time he went up. The four-seater plane seemed incredibly light and flimsy as it skimmed past the encroaching mountains, and Jinny's knuckles were white against the seat's dark plaid upholstery. Even the sight of Bret's long competent hands at the controls, and the knowledge that he had flown for years without mishap, did little to allay her fears.

'We're much too close to those ridges,' she gritted through her teeth. 'Can't you keep away from them?'

His grey eyes were amused when he glanced across at her rigidly held body on the seat next to his, and he put a casually reassuring hand on her knee. The warmth of it through the thick nylon of her slacks sent a shiver through her.

'Relax,' he advised, his even teeth showing whitely in a smile. 'I know what I'm doing—besides, I can't risk spooking your cows again when you're not there to dive into the mud after them, can I?'

It was the first reference he had made to his rescue of her from the lake and the ensuing scene at Valley Ranch. Never by even the flicker of an eye had he given the impression that he remembered her invitation for him to kiss her, and she was almost beginning to think it was a badly remembered dream herself. Now, however, the whole scene flashed across her eyes, and she fancied she could feel again the hard pressure of his mouth on hers, the practised caress of his capable hands that could control her responses to his lovemaking as effortlessly as they manipulated the plane's dials.

She heard his amused chuckle above the engine's noise, which seemed far less here than on the ground, and threw him a baleful look, contrarily feeling bereft when he lifted his hand from her knee and returned it to the control stick.

Something in his expression caught and held her attention. There was an alert yet carefree look about his eyes, a loose but controlled movement of his shoulders as he moved his arms to and from the panel in front of him, that spoke of complete relaxation. Jinny's own taut muscles were soothed when she saw that the lines normally etched deep into the space between his brows and round his eyes had been smoothed away until they were just faintly visible, as if he had left his troubles far beneath him on the ground.

Her eyes drew reluctantly away from him, and a cry of pleasure escaped her when she saw the rolling panorama of mountains and valley pastures passing lazily below.

'Look, Bret, aren't those your cows?'

She pointed eagerly to her right where, dotted along the verdant green of a side valley, white-faced Herefords cropped hungrily at the succulent grass.

'Uh-huh. Can you tell roughly how many there are?'

She looked calculatingly down and made a swift appraisal before the valley was lost to the rear of the plane. 'I'd say about two hundred and fifty—maybe three hundred.'

He whistled softly, and seemed pleased. 'As many as that? The losses couldn't have been as bad as Frank thought they might be. Of course, that's only a small part of the stock. Most of it lies quite a bit north of here, so they may not have fared so well over the winter.'

Excitement brought a deep shine to Jinny's eyes, and she settled into her seat in anticipation of the longer flight to check the movements of the larger herd. Disappointment cut sharply through her when Bret banked the small plane and made a turn to head back in the direction they had come from.

'Aren't you going to check on the others?' she asked in a small voice.

Bret shook his head. 'Not today. You've been far enough for the first time, and I don't want your grandfather worrying about you. I'll come up myself in a day or two when I've put my head together with Frank's and worked out where the stock's likely to be.'

His voice was friendly but impersonal, and Jinny sensed his wish to be alone when he took the longer trip. Feeling rebuffed, she sank back against the cushioned seat and said no more until he had made the bumpy landing on the hastily constructed airstrip near the ranch.

'Thank you,' she said politely as he helped her down from the cockpit, his hands warm under her arms. 'I enjoyed it.'

'Good.' For a moment he kept his hands where they were, then stepped away from her and said without conviction: 'You'll have to come again some time.'

But days passed into weeks and he made no further mention of her going with him again. Jinny's head was the only one raised at the O'Brien ranch when the familiar reverberations sounded across the Valley, and even Endor's harsh protests were heard less often as he settled to the raising of a new family high in the crags.

In late May, the Valley seemed permanently bathed in sunshine, and Jinny worried about whether to sell off some of the cattle now, when they were filling out to sleek plumpness, or to wait until the fall sales, when the animals would weigh more and bring in more money. Denis was of little help to her in the decision. As his health deteriorated, so his interest in ranch matters dwindled until Jinny stopped asking his advice and shouldered the entire burden herself.

One evening she sat at the open window in the living room, a book before her on the small table, but her eyes were directed to the gathering dusk beyond the window.

Bret and her grandfather had been silently concentrating on the chessmen for some time, and Jinny started when Bret's voice came from the other side of the table.

'Why so pensive?' he asked quietly, taking a thin cigar from his pocket and looking over a flaring match directly into her eyes. He saw her concerned glance towards her grandfather, and added in the same low tone: 'It's all right, he's asleep. I don't smoke in front of him, because I know he can't any more. I'll blow the smoke from the window so he won't smell it when he wakes up.'

'Thanks, Bret, that's—thoughtful of you.' To her horror, unbidden tears surged into her eyes and she blinked furiously to get rid of them as he leaned across to toss the match outside. The last thing she wanted was for Bret to think she was pulling a weak woman's trick to get his sympathy. By the time he dropped into the seat opposite, the tears had dispersed, leaving a luminous glow about her eyes in the half light.

'So what's bothering you?' he persisted, his eyes narrowed against a spiral of smoke from the cigar. 'You've been looking as if the end of the world was just around the corner since you sat down here. Is it your grandfather?'

Jinny shook her head. 'Not really, though——' She looked over again at the old man's bent head, afraid he would wake up and hear himself being discussed.

Bret stood up. 'Get yourself a sweater and we'll take a walk outside. He won't wake up for a while, and we won't be far away.'

Excitement tingled along her nerves as she rejoined him at the porch steps, a white wool sweater slung round her shoulders. That was how it would always be, she thought as they walked slowly towards the corral fence, this awareness of him in the slightest touch of his arm against hers, the silvery light reflected from a moon rising lazily from behind the mountains in his eyes.

He put a foot up on the paddock fence and said, his voice

hushed in keeping with the charmed stillness around them: 'Jinny, you—have you thought what you'll do when—your grandfather isn't here any more?'

The unexpectedness of his question startled her into saying, hurt: 'Pop will live for a long time yet. Lots of people who have had heart attacks live for years.'

'He's an old man, Jinny, and you're young. Sooner or later you'll have to——'

'I'll think about that when the time comes,' she snapped, pulling the dangling sleeves of her sweater round her arms. 'It's like wishing Pop dead to think of . . . after.'

'Don't be ridiculous. If wishing or thinking about it could kill people there would be very few left! It's only sensible to make plans for your life.'

'I *have* made plans,' she said fiercely. 'I plan to stay on this ranch for ever. Pop hasn't been able to help much lately, but I've—managed.'

'So what were you worried about in the house tonight? It wasn't your grandfather, you say, so it must be something to do with the ranch. Or is it that your policeman hasn't been around lately?' His eyes gleamed with sudden mockery, and she felt a quick desire to slap the taut smoothness of his jaw.

'Mike had nothing to do with what I was thinking about. As a matter of fact, I was wondering whether I should sell off some of the cattle now or wait until——'

'Sell now?' He was immediately all rancher. 'I wouldn't advise that, Jinny. Prices are just about at their lowest. Why don't you wait a while, or'—he frowned—'do you need the money?'

She was thankful that the cool moonlight hid the warm surge of colour to her cheeks. 'We can manage,' she said with dignity, looking up at him in surprise when his foot struck against the fence.

'I wish there was something I could do to help,' he said regretfully and with a touch of annoyance. 'But my capital's tied up in the ranch and plane business.'

'We wouldn't accept help anyway, Bret, but thanks for thinking of it. We'll get by.'

She turned to go back to the house, anxious about her grandfather, but his arm came across to stop her. The touch of his strong fingers on her elbow was enough to set her heart hammering wildly in her breast, and her breath drew inward with an audible sigh as she looked up into his face.

The moon's light illuminated his every feature, the smooth line of his tightly held jaw, the sharp rise of cheek-bone that gave him a hard-won maturity, but it was the fierce glitter in his eyes that held her as if hypnotised when his other hand came up to grasp her shoulder and draw her round to face him.

'There *is* a way we could solve your problems, Jinny,' he said in a voice that was oddly hoarse. 'You could——'

He hesitated, seeming to search for the right words, and seemed relieved when Denis's querulous voice called her name from the house. At the same time, a car's headlights loomed like huge cat's eyes from down the road which led only to the O'Brien ranch.

'Who in the world could that be?' Jinny wondered, her voice edged with irritation.

'You take care of the visitor,' Bret said precisely, already lengthening his stride towards the house. 'I'll see to your grandfather.'

She followed him more slowly to the porch, noting the almost relieved lift of his shoulders, and wondered what he had been about to say. Judging from his carefree air now, it was something he was glad not to have said.

A deeper frown crossed her brow when she turned from the porch and saw a uniformed Mike getting out of a police car. There was an official swing to his shoulders as he came over to greet her.

'Hi, Jinny. I'm glad I caught you out here. I wouldn't want your grandfather to be upset by what I have to say.'

'Why would Pop be upset at anything you have to say, Mike?' she asked with challenging irony, and for a moment his mouth compressed into a narrow line.

'We're on the lookout for two escapees from the penitentiary in Vancouver. They've been reported seen in this area, so we're warning everyone to lock up their homes securely for a day or two. They could be dangerous, Jinny, so be sure to lock your doors and windows, will you?' His blue eyes were shaded by the peak on his cap as he glanced over to the car he had parked beside, but his voice was laden with sarcasm when he added: 'I called at Valley Ranch and warned the housekeeper. I see now why Stafford wasn't there himself.'

'Bret's playing chess with Pop,' Jinny defended coolly.

'Oh? I thought I saw him out here walking with you.'

'Only while Pop was asleep—is that some kind of crime?'

'No,' he replied evenly, half turning away, then looking back as if in afterthought. 'It's Tom Field's retirement party this coming Friday. He particularly mentioned that he's expecting you to be there—will you come?'

'I'd love to go, Mike, but Pop needs me here at night.' Jinny's disappointment was sincere. She had known Tom Field, head of the R.C.M.P. Detachment at Gold Valley, for many years and had looked forward to his long-awaited retirement party.

'If there's something you want to attend, I'll stay with your grandfather, Jinny. It would do you good to get out of the house for a while.'

She whirled round at the sound of Bret's voice, wondering how much of the conversation he had heard and faintly resenting his unashamed eavesdropping.

'I couldn't let you do that,' she said haughtily.

'Why not?' Mike put in from behind. 'You're not needed when they're playing chess anyway, are you?' The sarcasm in his voice was unmistakable, and Jinny swung round to

face him again, a sharp retort forming on her lips, when
Bret spoke smoothly instead.

'Exactly. Let me know what time I'll be needed, will
you, Jinny? I'll be coming by some time tomorrow.' He
came down the steps. 'Your grandfather's more interested
in bed than chess right now. Goodnight, Jinny.'

He nodded to Mike and crossed to the Stafford car, Mike
excusing himself hurriedly to Jinny and following Bret,
standing at the open door of his car talking earnestly to
him. Jinny heard him repeat his warning about the prisoners, and then her grandfather called her and she went with a
sigh into the house. As an afterthought, she drew the heavy
bolts which hadn't been used for years across the front door,
leaning with her back to it for several minutes before going
into the living room.

If only Bret had not seemed so anxious for her to go out
with Mike to the retirement party! Surely any man, even
one uninterested in her as a woman, would be at least a
little reluctant to throw her into the arms of another man.
But Bret had been eager for her to go to the party on
Friday with Mike.

Again she wondered what it was he had been about to say
to her when her grandfather called. 'There is a way we
could solve your problems, Jinny. You could . . .'—*what?*

Before Bret came on Friday evening Jinny slipped on the
only full-length dress she possessed and surveyed herself
dispassionately in the bedroom mirror. The colour,
hyacinth blue, was a perfect match for her eyes, but the
rounded curves of her body had been fined down to slender
firmness since she had made the dress two years before, and
the fit was far from perfect.

But it would have to do, she decided with a sigh, dismissing from her mind's eye the vision of a pale blonde girl in
Bret's adoring arms, her exquisitely cut dress shimmering
under the lights of a blazing chandelier.

'Jinny? Better hurry it up—your policeman's here.'

The sound of Bret's voice through the door made her jump, and she swept up the white wool stole she had laid out on the bed and threw it on without answering. Why, oh, why did it have to be Bret Stafford standing outside her door? Would his eyes gleam with mockery at her lack of glamour? Or, worse still, reflect pity because he knew she was unable to dress as well as the other women he knew?

But the small hall was empty when she opened her door, and she was relieved to hear the murmur of male voices from outside. She went quickly into the living room, where her grandfather sat in his customary chair, noting with concern how tired he looked before he saw her and forced a twinkle into his blue eyes.

'Well, Jinny, you look beautiful, darlin',' he said fondly. 'You'll be the belle of the ball. I just wish it was Bret you were going out with, instead of that police fellow.'

Jinny dropped to her knees beside him and leaned across to kiss his lined cheek. 'So do I, Pop,' she smiled, whispering.

'Do you, Jinny?' He sighed contentedly when she nodded, her eyes shining like stars. 'Then I've done the right thing.'

'What do you mean, Pop?' She looked at him anxiously. Of late, his mind seemed to wander off course more than ever before. She stood up quickly when Bret's voice came from the doorway.

'Your escort's getting impatient, Jinny.'

'I'm coming.'

Jinny clasped her grandfather's hand again and had taken a few steps towards the door when she turned impulsively back to bend and kiss his cheek. 'I won't be late, Pop.'

'Enjoy yourself, darlin'. Be good.'

'I will, Pop.'

Bret scarcely glanced at her dress when she passed him in the doorway, but his eyes were solemn on hers as he said softly: 'Don't worry. I'll take care of him till you get back.'

For the second time within minutes, Jinny reached up impulsively to kiss a man's cheek—one lined with age, the other smooth and taut in youth.

'Thank you, Bret,' she whispered, and half ran from the house before he had time to register more than shocked surprise.

In spite of the gay decorations put up in honour of Tom Field in one of the smaller rooms at the Community Centre, Jinny felt little joy in the evening. Again and again, whether she was in Mike's or someone else's arms dancing, or toasting Tom's health as he beamed happily from a centre table, her thoughts went back to the two men she had left at Hillside Ranch. The two she loved.

'Glad you came, Jinny?' Mike smiled across the table at her, and she looked dazedly at him. His fair, strongly handsome face seemed like a stranger's to her. Why was she here with him, when all she wanted was to be with the two men she cared most about in the world? It didn't matter that one of them would never love her in the same way. As long as she could see the darkness of his head bent close to the white of her grandfather's over the chessboard, she would be happy.

'Mike, I——' She half rose from her seat, then sank back into it when a young constable, his uniform immaculately pressed, appeared beside them and bent to speak quietly to Mike.

'Okay, I'll be right there. Get Prudholme and Jones, will you?'

Mike was already on his feet, bending over Jinny to say tersely: 'Sorry, Jinny, but I'll have to leave you. The missing prisoners I told you about are holed up at the Talon place just outside town. I don't know how long it will take to get them out of there—seems they have guns. But I'll get back if I can.'

'Don't worry, Mike, I'll take a taxi home,' she assured him quickly, concern in her eyes as she looked up into his face with its new expression of remote efficiency. 'Be careful, Mike.'

A fleeting smile glinted ironically in his eyes. 'Would it matter to you if I wasn't? See you, Jinny.'

She watched his broad figure thread its way among the groups of people on the small dance floor and wished she could feel more than friendly concern for him.

'Where did Mike disappear to in such a hurry?'

Tom Field, the iron grey of his hair belying the warm brown of his eyes, dropped into the seat Mike had vacated.

'The escaped prisoners—they're at the Talon place,' Jinny explained absently, then saw the gleam of interest in the older policeman's eyes. 'They have guns, Mike said.'

Tom whistled softly. 'Hope they haven't harmed the old people. I'd sure like to be in on this, but'—he sighed—'I guess I've been put out to pasture.' Abruptly changing the subject, he asked: 'How are you getting home, Jinny? Mike probably won't be——'

'I told him I'd take a taxi. In fact, I think I'll go right now—I'm a little concerned about my grandfather.'

After enquiring about the old man, Tom said: 'Let me get a cab for you. There's not much else I can do to help Mike now.'

Business was slack for the two-car taxi company which Gold Valley boasted, and Jinny was soon being driven swiftly back to Hillside. Halfway there, a long black car passed on the other side of the narrow road, and Jinny said almost to herself: 'Who was that?'

'Looked like the Doc's car,' the driver shrugged. 'Maybe somebody's sick at Valley Ranch.'

Valley Ranch? The only person there tonight was Olive Trent, and she was the kind who never got sick. 'Hurry, please!' Jinny urged, cold fear clutching her heart.

CHAPTER FOUR

JINNY jumped from the taxi as it was still coming to a halt in front of the house. The driver waved away her offer of payment, saying it had been taken care of, and she stood, suddenly paralysed, as the blue and white cab circled the grassy oval and left.

The sight of Bret rising slowly from the porch steps where he had been sitting, tossing away the cigar in his hand, intensified the fear she had felt after glimpsing the doctor's car. Bret made no move to come to her and she forced her feet to cover the few yards between them.

'I—saw the doctor's car. Did Pop have another attack?'

'Yes, Jinny,' he said heavily. 'He——'

'I must go in to him.' She moved to brush past him, but his hand came out to grasp her arm and turn her back to face him. Now she noticed the strained pallor on his face, the raw hurt in his eyes.

'No. You can't do any more for him now, Jinny. Do you—understand?'

Denial fought with knowledge of what he was saying and she felt a cold numbness spread across her brain. As from a distance, Bret's arms reached out to catch her when she swayed, his hand pressing her head to his shoulder, his fingers smoothing her hair with a wordless, rhythmical motion. Unable to accept the emotional reality of his words, her other senses seemed pitched to a much higher reception than normal. Every fibre of his jacket impressed itself on the soft skin of her cheek, and underneath the faint scent of the cologne he used she discerned the warm, fresh odour of his skin.

'Why did it have to happen when I wasn't here?' she whispered brokenly against his neck. 'Why didn't you call me, Bret?'

'There was nothing you could have done, Jinny,' he told her gently. 'He was talking ... about you ... one minute, and the next he was gone. It was very peaceful.'

Dry-eyed, she pulled herself from his arms. 'I'm glad of that. But I'd still have liked to be with him.'

His eyes searched her face, grown deadly pale in the moonlight glinting across from the mountain top behind them. A subdued whinny came from one of the horses, left out overnight in the pasture beside the stables.

'The doctor left some sleeping pills for you. I want you to get right into bed, and I'll bring you a hot drink to take with them.'

Jinny, too numb to demur, accepted the command in his voice and turned obediently into the house. The door to her grandfather's bedroom was closed tight, something it had not been since his illness because Jinny had been anxious to hear if he called in the night.

'Get into bed,' Bret said again. 'I'll be back in a few minutes.'

He went out, closing the door softly behind him, and in a daze Jinny moved to take off her dress and hang it neatly, by force of habit, in the closet. When Bret tapped on the door a few minutes later and came in bearing a steaming cup of milky chocolate, she found nothing odd in the fact that she was propped against the pillows in her high-necked blue nightdress while he came to sit on the edge of the double bed she had once shared with Lesli.

'Take these,' he said, holding out two pink pills on the palm of his hand, watching with steady grey eyes while she swallowed them. 'I'll stay in the house tonight, Jinny, in the living room. Call me if you need me. Drink up now.'

He took the cup from her when she had drained it, and sat watching her quietly for several minutes as she stared up at the ceiling. She tried to force her mind to the realisation that Pop was dead, that she would never hear his voice again or see the flashing blue of his Irish eyes, but she could feel nothing. Perhaps tomorrow ... The pills must be fast acting, she thought, her eyelids beginning to feel heavy ... Bret's face was growing dim round the edges, but the desolate look there reminded her of the time when she had told him Lesli had eloped with Eddie Clark.

'Were you very hurt, Bret, when Lesli went away?' she whispered. 'You went away the very next day, so you must ...'

Forcing her lips open, she saw him frown as if in remembered anguish, and his voice came from far away.

'It was a long time ago, Jinny. I can't remember what I felt then.'

Her eyes closed and she barely felt the touch of his hands on her hips under the covers as they pulled her down on the bed, or the arranging of pillows under her head. What made her struggle for awareness was the touch of his lips on her forehead—lips that had none of the dry hardness of his kisses and Valley Ranch, but which were instead warm with compassion and ...

Birds were singing in joyful anticipation of the coming day when Jinny opened her eyes again. Light filtered unevenly through the open weave mesh of her bedroom curtains and she lay listening to the familiar sounds of morning. A rooster proclaimed with proud arrogance his sovereignty over the henhouses and runs in his province, and from the cowshed came the gentle lowing of Maura, the milk cow. Strange how Pop had named so many of the domestic animals after people he had known long ago in Ireland, she reflected. Pop! ...

Remembrance flooded back to one part of her mind, but other segments of her brain moved quickly to block the pain memory brought and she began to calculate with cool detachment the tasks she must perform that day. Maura must be milked, the horses groomed and fed—but first, coffee. Throwing back the covers, Jinny jumped out of bed and dressed quickly in warm navy sweater and slim blue jeans before going out to the kitchen.

The cup that had held her hot drink the night before had been rinsed and set upside down on the draining board, reminding her through the heavy dullness in her head that Bret had said something about staying the night. She threw coffee into the battered aluminium pot and filled it with water at the tap, placing it on the stove at low heat while she went across to the living room.

Her eyes automatically avoided her grandfather's empty chair, seeking and finding instead Bret's long figure on the sofa beyond it. Her feet in soft shoes made no sound as she went to stand beside the sleeping man, his body cramped into a tortuous position on the small sofa. He had pushed a cushion under his head, and one arm was extended over the edge, fingers curved slightly over the upturned palm. Lashes longer than any man's had a right to be rested in a dark smudge above the tanned skin of his cheekbones, and a beginning growth of beard shadowed the strong thrust of his chin.

His breath sounded with quiet regularity in the stillness of the room, and there was a defenceless quality about him that wrenched her heart. There seemed to be no connection between the innocent-looking Bret on the sofa and the man whose ambition had driven him to the top of a competitive business and brought into his life the women anxious to satisfy his needs. Jinny's hand made a compulsive motion towards the thick darkness of his hair, then dropped to her side again.

She had collected the eggs from the henhouses and relieved a grateful Maura of her milk before Bret appeared in the kitchen doorway, his hair rumpled but eyes alert as they watched her pour coffee into man-size mugs.

'Sorry, Jinny,' he said with early morning brevity. 'I meant to bring coffee to you this morning.'

'Why should you?' she asked calmly, placing his mug at

one side of the small table where she usually ate her breakfast. 'I had a wonderful night's sleep, and that's more than you had on the sofa.'

He looked closely into her composed features as he took the chair opposite hers, putting cream and sugar into his coffee with a thoughtful expression on his face. He said nothing, however, until he had placed his empty mug on the yellow and white checked cloth.

'Jinny,' he began hesitantly, 'you remember what happened last night, and why I stayed here?'

'Of course,' she replied matter-of-factly. 'Pop——'

The sound of a motor-cycle coming along the road to the ranch brought her to her feet with an exclamation.

'I'd forgotten this is Saturday—Tommy Stiles comes to help out today. I'll send him home.'

Bret caught her arm and rose as she rushed past his chair. 'I'll see him while you finish your coffee. Is there nothing he can do now he's here?'

'I've seen to everything except the horses, but . . .'

He had gone without waiting to hear her objection, and when Tommy's motor stopped seconds later she heard the hushed murmur of their voices, Tommy's rising to a higher pitch just before Bret reappeared in the kitchen.

'You realise you'll have to marry me now!' she said lightly, throwing him a brittle smile as she refilled his coffee cup and added to her own. 'Tommy's a great bearer of gossip, and when it gets around town that you——'

'Stop it, Jinny!' Bret's hands were hard on her shoulders, shaking her so that her hair fell back and forth across her face. 'You're in a state of shock or you'd never think of people questioning my motives for staying overnight. Besides,' he let her go and went to sit down, 'they've more exciting things to talk about than where I spent the night. They've caught those escaped prisoners after a siege lasting half the night.'

Collapsing into her own chair, she said dully: 'Oh yes,

I'd forgotten about that. Some of the fellows had to leave the party last night.'

Was it only last night she had gone to the retirement party with Mike? Nothing seemed real to her this morning, perhaps because of the pills Bret had given her. They had ensured a deep and dreamless sleep, but had left her feeling strangely detached from her surroundings, her emotions deadened. It was even an effort to drag her attention back to what Bret was saying.

'... got them, but one of the policemen was injured.' He paused before going on carefully: 'It was Mike Preston, Jinny.'

She stared at him uncomprehendingly. 'Mike? Mike was hurt?'

'Not badly. A shoulder wound, but he'll be in hospital for a week or so, I'd guess.'

'Oh.' She sighed. 'That's too bad.' Mike had been hurt, yet she could feel nothing more than if Bret had passed a remark about the weather.

He said quietly: 'We have to let Lesli know, Jinny, about your grandfather. Do you have an address for her?'

'Who? Oh—Lesli.' She shook her head as if coming out of a trance. 'I don't have a permanent address for her, she's never in one place long enough. But she wrote once that she could be reached through the—the Racing Circuit head office in Florida. I have that address somewhere.'

Bret followed her into the living room and stood behind her while she searched in the desk for the scrap of paper Lesli had sent years before. She found it at last tucked away at the back of a drawer, and turned to hand it to him. Without a glance at Lesli's bold script scrawled across it, he put the paper inside his wallet and restored it to his hip pocket. Jinny wondered detachedly if that meant he had got over the love he had once had for her sister, but the thought faded almost before it arose. Even Bret's love life failed to stir her lethargic senses this morning.

'I'll send off a telegram,' he was saying when she focused her attention on him again. 'If she's in the States somewhere, she should be able to make it back in time.'

'Thanks, Bret. I—I don't know what I'd do without your help.'

He caught her hands in his and, when she looked up at him in surprise, said urgently: 'You're going to need a man's help now, Jinny. You can't run this place on your own, or even live alone in this house. I know it's not the right time to speak about this'—his eyes went to her grandfather's closed door—'but it's what he wanted too, I think. Will you marry me, Jinny?'

Shock deepened the dark blue pools of her eyes as she stared up at him. 'M-marry you? But——'

'I'm not asking for an answer now,' he said almost brusquely. 'Just that you keep it in mind and think about it for a while. Will you do that?'

She nodded dumbly, her eyes seeming to cling as if mesmerised to his, watching as his head bent to kiss first her cheek and then her lips. His felt warm against the icy numbness of hers, his eyes tender when he straightened and looked at her.

Not until many days had passed would she be able to assess those moments when he had asked her to be his wife. Now she struggled to feel, and knew nothing but calm acceptance of yet another shock in her life.

The numbed composure that had fallen on her after grandfather's death remained with Jinny through the trying days that followed. She was vaguely aware of the whispers between neighbours who came in to help and support her, of their shock at her dry-eyed command of herself when they had expected tears. Tommy Stiles' mother, who stayed with Jinny at the ranch, left after three nights and declared to her town cronies that the O'Brien girl was 'unnatural' in her lack of grief.

Even a last-minute telegram from Lesli saying 'Sorry impossible get away letter follows'—as if she had been invited to a weekend house party—failed to penetrate the icy barrier round Jinny's feelings.

Cause for speculation, too, was the presence of Bret at Hillside Ranch whenever the well-meaning neighbours called there. Eyebrows were raised and looks exchanged when, without being asked, he would go to the kitchen and reappear a short time later with a tray of cups and well-made coffee or tea. He ignored the curious glances, seeming amused by them, but often when Jinny looked up she found his smoke-grey eyes watching her speculatively.

On such occasions her mind would veer away from the sympathetic murmurings around her to an inner remembrance of Endor. The eagle had, since her grandfather's death, forsaken his former shyness of the homestead and could be seen most mornings circling high up against the azure blue of the sky, borne lazily along on the winds that swept down the Valley at that altitude. Then with a sudden graceful swoop he would plunge to earth, settling into immobility on the paddock fence while smaller birds twittered a hasty retreat. Something in the unblinking watchfulness of Endor's yellow eyes reminded Jinny of the waiting look in Bret's. Waiting for the answer she had been unable to give him ...

Before long, Endor would rise again with a raucous squawk and a powerful spreading of his immense wings and return to the territory that was familiar to him. Jinny sensed that sooner or later Bret would feel that same need to return to his other environment, the one she knew nothing of. How long would the slow, peaceful way of life in Gold Valley hold his interest? One year? Two?

Ten days after the funeral, Bret was called back to Vancouver to attend to problems with the charter business which only he could handle, and for the first time Jinny felt the cold breeze of loneliness. Mary Stiles had gone, the other neighbours had paid their duty calls, and work about the ranch occupied much less of her time since Bret had sent one of his men over to see to the more arduous tasks.

So it came as a relief when, two days after Bret had left, she saw a car making its way to the ranch after lunch. A pang of guilt went through her when she recognised the car as Mike's. She had meant to visit him in hospital, which was some fifty miles from the small community of Gold Valley, but the opportunity—or, if she was honest, the desire to do so—never seemed to arise. Now she saw that Mike held his left shoulder stiffly as he got from the car, and that his face seemed paler than normal when he came towards her at the porch steps.

'Hello, Jinny,' he said gruffly, and put his good arm round her waist to draw her to him. He kissed her cheek lightly. 'Sorry about your grandfather—and sorrier still that I wasn't able to be of help to you.'

'And I'm sorry I didn't get into the hospital to see you, Mike,' she said penitently. 'Are you really better now?'

'Must be. The doctors let me drive a car today. Say, do you mind if we go inside? The sun's pretty hot out here.'

'No, of course I don't mind,' she agreed quickly, but nonetheless felt resentful when he went confidently past her to open the door and follow her into the house her grandfather had never welcomed him to.

'Not in that chair, Mike!' she called sharply when he crossed to the wing-backed chair old Denis had always used, and Mike raised his eyebrows but went to sit instead on the sofa beyond it. 'Would you like some coffee or tea?'

'I'd appreciate something a little stronger if you have it, Jinny. This shoulder feels like toothache most of the time.'

'Yes, of course.' She hesitated in the doorway. 'There's only a little of the brandy I used to give—Pop in his tea.'

'That would be fine,' he smiled, and she went hurriedly into the kitchen, feeling suddenly suffocated by his presence in the house. Her fingers shook as she took the brandy bottle from the cupboard, but she forced herself to calmness by the thought that perhaps Mike would go when he had drunk it.

He had risen and was prowling restlessly round the room when she came back. Taking the glass from her hand, he swallowed the short measure of dark liquid in one gulp and set the glass down on the table before turning to her.

'It must have been tough for you, handling everything yourself,' he said casually, yet Jinny detected a more intent purpose in his tone.

'I managed. Bret Stafford's been wonderful.'

'That's what I heard.' Mike's mouth tightened to a hard line. 'There's quite a lot of talk in town about you and him, Jinny.' His voice took on an even flatness. 'They're even saying he spends his nights here with you.'

Jinny gasped, anger flashing momentarily in her eyes, but she was icily controlled when she retorted: 'Bret spent one night here, yes. He slept on that sofa the night my grandfather died, so I wouldn't be alone in the house. I doubt if even the Gold Valley gossips would credit him with lustful intentions under those circumstances!' She turned away with a disgusted lift of her shoulders.

'Jinny, I'm sorry.' Mike stretched out an arm and drew her round to face him again, a shamed redness creeping under his skin. 'I should have known better than to listen to it. It just drove me crazy knowing he was here with you when I——' He broke off, then added with a serious frown: 'Jinny, I still want to marry you. Does it make any difference now that your grandfather can't come between us?'

'No difference whatsoever, Mike,' she said coldly, wrenching her arm away. 'I'm not in love with you.'

His ear picked up the faint emphasis on 'you' and his chin pushed forward angrily.

'You're still hankering after Stafford, aren't you? Good God, Jinny, don't you know it's a waste of time mooning

over a man like him? I've seen his kind over and over
again. He likes women for what he can get from them, and
drops them like hot potatoes whenever marriage is mentioned.'

'Does he really?' Jinny flared defensively, rushing on
without thinking: 'It so happens that Bret has asked me to
marry him—and I mean to accept him!'

Mike's jaw dropped, his blue eyes suddenly prominent as
he stared disbelievingly at her. Jinny could have felt sorry
for him, but she was so appalled by her own unwitting
declaration that she was stunned into silence.

'He—*what*?' Mike gasped.

Jinny stared back at his incredulous face without really
seeing it. She had said she was going to marry Bret! As if
saying the words had released the lock on her emotions,
feeling swept over her in an engulfing stream and overcame
her so much that she had to sit dazedly on a chair by the
window, scarcely able to make sense of the words Mike was
speaking behind her.

'Jinny, for God's sake don't rush into something you
might regret for the rest of your life. Bret Stafford's not the
husband for a girl like you! He'd break your heart, sooner
or later. He'll never be a one-woman man, Jinny, he's too
used to variety. Even in the short time he's been here he's
had a string of women out to the ranch. Carol's been out
there more than once, and I'd like to bet it wasn't to look at
his cows! He's had one of his fancy girl-friends down from
Vancouver for a weekend——' He broke off and looked
almost triumphantly at her shocked face. 'You didn't know
about that, did you? Mrs Trent's been there for more than
thirteen years and even she can't stomach what's going on
any more. She's leaving the Valley next week. Is *that* the
kind of husband you want, Jinny?'

'I love Bret,' she said simply, turning to look from the
window again. 'I think I always have, even when he and
Lesli——'

'There it is again,' he interrupted impatiently. 'What are you, Jinny, some kind of masochist? You can't love a man unless he makes you suffer? And believe me, that's exactly what Bret Stafford will make you do!' Mike came over to touch her shoulder, going on more softly: 'Jinny, I love you and I want to marry you. You'd have none of that heartache with me.'

'I'm sorry, Mike,' she said, a catch in her voice. 'It wouldn't be fair to marry you, loving someone else the way I do.'

His hand fell away from her shoulder and he stood looking down at her for long moments. Her dark head was bent so that her hair swung across her palely outlined cheek, and at last he sighed.

'I guess that's it, then. I'll—be around if you need me, Jinny.' Mike paused at the door to look back and say: 'I'd just like to know what Stafford has to gain by marrying you. I hope for your sake that all he's after is a loving wife!'

His well-set figure seemed dreamlike to Jinny as she watched him leave the house and get into his car. Fragments of his conversation played like a record over and over in her head. 'Carol's been out there more than once ... not to look at his cows ... fancy girl-friend from Vancouver for a weekend ... didn't know, did you? ... didn't know ...'

The eyes of love she turned upon Bret's behaviour told her that these other women didn't matter, they were unimportant to him except as a means of assuaging the loneliness of a single man. An instinct rooted deep in her emotions urged that no one had mattered to him since Lesli, his first love. And Lesli was a dream in his past, unattainable since her marriage to Eddie Clark. By marrying Bret, Jinny could free him from the earlier love for her sister ... couldn't she?

If only Pop were here, she thought, turning her sun-dazzled eyes towards his chair and fancying she saw the faint wisps of white hair and piercing blue of his eyes there. He would know what to say to comfort her, to assuage the fears underlying her decision to marry Bret.

'Pop? Oh, Pop!' Without realising quite how she got there, she found herself kneeling beside her grandfather's chair as she had so many times in the past, her arms stretched across it where his frail figure would have been. Tears that seemed to rise from the very depth of her being shook her slender body as she poured out the grief that had been stored up inside her.

She moaned when hands, masculine in their hardness, gripped her shoulders.

'Go away, Mike, please. I've told you—I'm going to marry Bret.'

'I'm very glad to hear that,' said a voice that was not Mike's, and the hands raised her from the floor and turned her to a blurred mid-grey business suit with matching tie and startlingly white shirt.

'Bret? Oh, Bret, you're back!'

As a child reaches for comfort to a sympathetic adult, so Jinny's arms went up round Bret's neck, her head burrowing against his chest. Without a word, he bent and scooped her into his arms, carrying her to an armchair where he sat down with her on his lap. Her head lay in the curve of his shoulder and her tears flowed again as if they would never stop. Shaking out the folds of an immaculate white handkerchief, he thrust it into her hand, his voice coming in a soothing murmur from above while he stroked the silky darkness of her hair with gentle fingers.

'There, baby, there . . . get it out, honey, that's better . . .'

His crooning went on until her pent-up grief was exhausted and only an occasional hiccup came in a sob against his neck. At last she pulled her head up, the handkerchief a sodden mass in her hand, and dropped her eyes from the tender compassion in his. If only Mike and the Gold Valley gossips could see him like this, she thought, her heart beginning to beat in an uneven tattoo when she became aware of the hard muscles of his thighs beneath her, the warmth of his body through the summer suiting he wore. Stealing a glance upwards through her lashes, she marvelled at the closeness of his sculptured mouth and finely shaped nose beneath eyes that looked without seeing into the white haze of sunlight pouring through the window. When those eyes came slowly to meet the tear-darkened orbs of hers, she felt the inevitability of his head bending and his lips touching hers, gently and compassionately at first and then moving with rising feeling back and forth. There was sudden impatience in his lifting of her hand to place it behind his neck, and limitless patience in the light touch of his hand caressing the length of her bare arm over and over.

Conscious only of the sensations arising deep within her, sensations that were half pain, half pleasure, she made no demur when his fingers went to the buttons on her blouse, sighing when his hand, warm and supple, cupped the soft curve of her breast. Emptied of grief, her emotional slate wiped clean, she was more than willing to have Bret write these new desires, new longings, there.

He raised his head to look searchingly into her eyes and the spectre of other women in his life faded when she saw the tense whiteness round his mouth, the flare of his nostrils as his breath hurried through them. A smile, born of confidence in her new-found ability to move him as she was sure no other woman could, trembled at the corners of her mouth and lit the blue of her eyes to shimmering softness.

'Jinny, I . . .' His voice was no more than a hoarse gasp and he seemed about to kiss her again when the sound of a pick-up truck came from outside. He cursed softly and said: 'Are you expecting anyone?'

Jinny shook her head in the negative, still mesmerised by his nearness and feeling unaccountably bereft when he rose hastily to deposit her on her feet.

'Bret? You here?'

Frank Milner's voice seemed loud in the stillness after the pick-up's engine was cut off. Bret, making a gesture for Jinny to stay where she was, walked to the door, straightening his tie and smoothing his hair as he went.

Jinny heard his feet on the porch, then Frank's purposely even voice.

'Thought I'd find you here. There was a call from your Vancouver outfit. Sounds urgent—they want you to call back right away.'

'Thanks. I'll be along in a minute.' There was a slight pause, then Bret's voice asking coldly: 'Something wrong with the way I look, Frank?'

The older man chuckled. 'No. It just beats me how you can wear a suit and tie on a day like this. Doesn't it cramp your style at all?'

'I manage,' Bret returned tersely. 'Thanks for bringing the message.'

Dismissed, Frank got back into the truck, and when its roar had faded to a faint hum in the distance Bret returned to the living room frowning.

'I'd forgotten how they thrive on gossip here,' he said with bitterness. 'Before nightfall, they'll all know I was here making love to you in my city suit.'

'I don't think it's Frank you should be concerned about.' Jinny moved at last from where he had left her earlier and went to stand close to the window. Apart from knowing that her face must look a mess after the deluge of tears, she had no wish to see his expression after her next words, which she knew she had to say. 'Mrs Trent has been telling anyone who'll listen that you've had—a number of girls— women—out at Valley Ranch.' Her hands tightened convulsively on the chair back in front of her. It was hardly likely the housekeeper had left out the juicy bit about Jinny herself having been there alone with him in the living room with only an oversized man's robe between her and her nudity.

'Oh?' Bret's voice was cold again. 'Who, for instance? Or did she just give me a blanket endorsement for the entire female population of Gold Valley?'

Jinny flushed. 'No. She mentioned Carol and a—a friend from Vancouver.'

'She didn't happen to mention, I suppose, that Carol Holmes came at her own invitation, not mine, on each of the two occasions she visited me?' he asked drily. 'Or that the "friend from Vancouver" is also my secretary who came here to work with me that weekend? We had expected her husband, who's also my chief pilot, to join us, but he was delayed up north by bad weather. Karen's a very attractive woman, but her husband's a good friend of mine and I'd like to keep it that way. Any more?'

She shook her head. 'No,' she said in a small voice. 'Unless you count me.'

'Oh yes, you.' A faint smile tinged his lips. 'As I recall it, you were the straw that broke the camel's—or I should say Mrs Trent's—back!'

'Oh no!' Jinny's head swivelled round, but her eyes dropped from the cool amusement in his. 'I guess I—I should have expected that. She has everybody convinced that you—spend your nights here.'

He said nothing for a moment or two, then stepped forward to turn her round to face him. 'Does it bother you that much? That they say things that aren't so?'

She shrugged, refusing to meet his level gaze. 'I don't know, Bret. It makes me feel uncomfortable when I know I'm being gossiped about. It—it's never happened to me before. You're used to it, I suppose.'

'I don't worry about people who speculate on my behaviour and come up with the wrong answers,' he corrected, moving away from her. 'But if it bothers you, we'll be married as soon as possible. Can you make it for next week?—say Friday?'

Her eyes opened wide as she stared at him. So, she imagined, would he cut through business red tape and get right to the point. Was marriage just another business problem to be surmounted?

'I ... suppose so,' she said slowly, adding with a helpless lift of her shoulders: 'I'll have to—buy things for it.' None of the clothes she had would be in any way suitable for the wife of Bret Stafford.

He laughed lightly and came to put his arms loosely round her. 'That's no problem. I think Valley Ranch can run to a dress or two for its future mistress!'

She looked up at him, hesitation in her expression. 'Bret, wouldn't it be better if Hillside was sold? If Lesli would agree, of course, because Pop left half of it to her.'

'No!' he said with a sharp frown. 'I don't think it would be a good idea to sell the place—in fact, I'm hoping I can persuade Lesli to sell her half if she and her husband come to visit this summer. She did say they might do that, didn't she, when she wrote?'

Jinny nodded. 'Yes, but ...' It was true Lesli had written a brief note after hearing of their grandfather's death, mentioning the possibility of a visit later, but then she had been promising that for years.

As if sensing her thoughts, Bret said: 'Even if they don't, we can get in touch with her—I don't imagine she wants to be saddled with half a property away up here.' He looked down seriously at Jinny. 'You know my father tried to buy Hillside for years, but your grandfather would never sell. I have great plans for Hillside, Jinny, and I think you'll agree when I tell you, but I don't intend to do that now. I haven't thought it all through yet.' He lifted an arm and glanced at his watch. 'I'd better get back and make that phone call. See you some time tomorrow, honey.'

For a moment, as his lips touched hers in a light kiss that

was far removed from the passion he had shown earlier, doubt clouded Jinny's eyes. Yet she was sure he loved her. Her body still flamed with the desire he had sparked from his own obvious need. But she would have to realise that business would always come first with him. Everything else, even his deepest personal needs, would be subordinated to that.

CHAPTER FIVE

JINNY'S initial reaction to Vancouver's bustling streets and towering buildings was one of excited exhilaration. Stores filled with the latest fashions abounded, bewildering her with styles that would not reach Gold Valley for months, if ever. Sympathy flowed from her towards the strained-looking people who hurried along the streets as if their lives depended on the business taking them there.

Bret had allowed her this one day for shopping before their civil ceremony wedding on Friday afternoon. It had been late on Wednesday afternoon when they flew into the city, and Bret had rushed straight from plane to car and driven to her hotel without stopping to show her round the huge hangar which housed his planes.

The stores he had recommended to her had revealed his taste in women's clothes. All were sophisticatedly conservative and expensive beyond her wildest imaginings. Even the minimum of what she considered necessary for Bret's bride amounted to an astronomical sum, and she was thankful that a speedy sale of some of the O'Brien cattle enabled her to meet the expense herself without delving into the cash Bret had put at her disposal.

On her way back to the Carillon Hotel, footsore and weary after a full day's trek round the stores, she caught a glimpse of her new hairdo in a shop window and wished for a moment that she could put up a hand to touch the crisply shorn curls. But both arms were fully occupied with small packages—the larger ones had been sent on to the hotel. Several of the men who passed her on the sidewalk cast admiring glances in her direction, and she wondered if Bret's eyes would light up in the same way. She wasn't at all sure if he would appreciate, as the French hair-stylist had, the highlighting of her cheekbones with jet black wisps of hair curled seductively round them, or the new prominence of her dark-fringed eyes.

The truth was, she thought as she stared unseeingly into a shop window filled with fishing tackle, that she really didn't know Bret well enough to gauge what would please him or not. Several times during the past week doubts had crept into her mind, doubts that were hard to dispel when she was near him and sensed his preoccupation with other things. Only the occasional relaxed smile coming as a sun-ray across the light grey of his eyes caused her confidence to surge again, particularly when he drew her into his arms to kiss her with an ardour that promised undreamed-of fulfilment to come.

Now her feet sank gratefully into the thick carpeting of the Carillon Hotel's lobby. She was looking forward to a soak in the tub before dressing for dinner with Bret. Several of the diners in the hotel's dining room had recognised him last night as he led her to a corner table for two, and Jinny had felt curious female eyes scrutinising her ill-fitting blue dress, though Bret had seemed oblivious to the raised brows. Tonight she would wear the expensively slender cream dress with boat neckline, and maybe the . . .

Her thoughts were abruptly terminated when a familiarly tall figure detached itself from one of the pillars leading to the lounge area.

'Bret! I thought you wouldn't be here until dinner!' Jinny's delighted smile faded when she saw the annoyed frown between Bret's dark brows.

'What have you done to your hair?' he asked in a voice that was half disbelieving, half disapproving.

'Don't you like it?' she asked tremulously, wishing again that she could put up a hand to touch the sculptured waves.

'I liked you better the way you were,' he said shortly. 'You look like any other girl around town now.'

Deflated, Jinny looked helplessly up into his eyes and a gleam of compassion lit the stormy grey.

'I guess I'll get used to the new you,' he said more gently, bending to kiss her cheek but finding the parcels coming between them. With a turn of his head towards the reception desk and a half lift of one eyebrow he brought a uniformed boy running to their side. 'Take these things up to Miss O'Brien's room, will you?'

The boy departed with the packages and a generous tip, and Bret took Jinny's elbow to lead her to the dimly lit bar tucked away behind the reception area.

'I came by to tell you that I won't be able to have dinner with you tonight, Jinny. Some business has come up that I have to attend to.'

'Oh.' Disappointment was evident in Jinny's voice and suddenly drooping shoulders. So much for dazzling him with her new dress!

'I'm sorry, honey,' he said as he settled her at a corner table near the door, where an amber-shaded wall sconce was their only illumination. 'Believe me, I'd rather spend the evening with you than with——' He broke off and asked what she would like to drink as a waiter bent over their table. 'It could be important to our future,' he went on when the white-coated man had retreated again into the gloom. 'When it's all settled, I'll explain it to you.'

Their drinks were brought in a remarkably short time, and Jinny drank thirstily from her long cool one encrusted with ice chips. Knowing Bret had dismissed business as a subject not fit for her ears, she spent the next ten minutes recounting her experiences in the stores he had recom-

mended, extracting as much humour as possible from the
fragmented impressions remaining with her, and feeling
rewarded when his facial muscles relaxed and his teeth
glinted faintly in the subdued light from above. It was
strange, she thought wonderingly, how he could suddenly
revert to the carefree self of his youth. Here in these alien
surroundings, far from Gold Valley, she glimpsed the Bret
he had been long ago.

As if in keeping with the lighthearted air between them,
he lit a cigar and took the embossed band encircling it into
his long fingers. Lifting her right hand, he looked solemn as
he slid the slender band on to her third finger and said:
'That should hold you until tomorrow.'

'Wrong hand,' she said lightly.

'I thought it was the right one.'

'It is,' she explained, laughter making her voice un-
steady. 'But it's the wrong one just the same.'

'Oh.' He looked pensive for a moment, then his hand
went down to delve into his jacket pocket. 'Well, as I only
smoke one cigar at a time, maybe this will do for the other
one.' His thumb flipped open the lid of a red leather box to
reveal an exquisitely set solitaire diamond ring. Jinny
gasped as he slid it along her finger, where it fitted in snug
perfection as if finding the home intended for it.

'It's—it's beautiful, Bret,' she breathed, raising shining
eyes from the diamond to his face. 'But it looks horribly
expensive.'

He put back his head and laughed, then reached over to
clasp both of her hands in his, the ring feeling strange
against her flesh when his hand covered it. 'Jinny darling,
you're the most unusual girl I've ever met! We're not even
married yet, but already you're acting like a thrifty wife.'
More soberly, he added: 'The Stafford fortunes can run to
an engagement ring, honey. And soon I hope you'll never
feel you have to be thrifty again.' He looked at his watch,
taking his hands away from hers. 'I'm sorry, Jinny, but I'll

have to go and get changed at the apartment. Why don't you have dinner in your room and then an early night? Honeymoons are notorious for robbing people of sleep.'

His voice had dropped half a notch with the last words, and despite herself Jinny blushed, thankful that the sub-dued lighting disguised the fact. Friends of Bret's were providing a beach cottage on Vancouver Island for a week's honeymoon, and the thought of being alone with this man of many parts, the sole recipient of his attention, was enough to reduce her to quivering nervousness.

In her room later, she scarcely touched the well-cooked meal wheeled into her room on a trolley. Toying with the charcoal-broiled steak, and eating most of the tossed salad accompanying it, she wondered where Bret was at that moment. Probably closeted in some austere office negotiat-ing a charter deal for the airline. The business world was an alien planet to her. No wonder Bret preferred the unhurried pace of life in Gold Valley, where business was conducted in daylight hours and a man could be master of his own domain when night fell. Here, the work day seemingly ex-tended far into the night. Traffic still moved in a never-ending stream beneath her window—where did all the people in those cars go?

In bed at last, Jinny tried to read the book she had bought in the hotel's lobby shop, but after several futile attempts laid it on the night table and switched off the bedside lamp. By this time tomorrow she would be Mrs Bret Stafford ... Jinny Stafford. She rolled the syllables round her tongue and felt pleased with their effect. Mrs Stafford ... Bret's wife ... wife ...

Would the love she felt for him in every pore be enough for the man who had known sophisticated women, women skilled in the most intimate relationship there could be be-tween a man and a woman?

The bridal suite at the Carillon must have been designed by

someone dedicated to romance, Jinny thought as she leaned on the balcony overlooking the twinkling lights of a city still active. Behind her, through sliding glass doors, lay the suite's sitting room with its furniture of oyster satin upholstery, the painstakingly arranged bowls of sweetheart roses on tables and desk, the thick rug which invited the touch of bare toes.

In daylight, the suite commanded an astounding view of the thousand-acre Stanley park and the ribbon of Pacific inlet behind it. It was towards the furthest point, the North Shore mountains, that Jinny's eyes now strained, although nothing was visible except the golden line of lights outlining Grouse Mountain ski trail. Imagining the cool freshness of the slopes, Jinny shivered in her low-cut negligée of white lace, starting when Bret's arms encircled her waist from behind.

'Come inside, Jinny darling,' he whispered against her ear, sending tremors that had nothing to do with the chilly air racing across her skin. 'You're shivering.'

His lips traced the line of her softly moulded jaw and reached for her mouth, turning her in his arms to do so. His body radiated warmth through the silky grey-striped robe he wore, and she clung mindlessly to it for animal comfort and reassurance while her lips remained stiff under the gentle movement of his. His eyes gleamed more green than grey in the soft radiance of light coming from the sitting room when he raised his head to look searchingly at her paled complexion.

'What's the matter, Jinny?' he asked huskily, lifting a hand to smooth the hair away from her temple. 'Having regrets already?'

'No,' she denied quickly, but her eyes dropped to the dark chest hair curling from between the edges of his robe, finding that proof of his masculinity increasing her nervousness so that her voice was oddly contorted when she added: 'Bret, I—it's just that—I'm not as experienced as——'

His soft laugh cut off her words and he pulled her towards him and said against her hair: 'You funny little thing, is that what's bothering you? Don't you know that I'm selfish enough to want to be the one to teach you? And that I wouldn't object if that took the rest of my life?'

'Oh, Bret, I love you so much,' she whispered, her eyes darkened to navy as she reached up to kiss his freshly shaved cheek and then, shyly, the clear-cut line of his lips. His arms tightened round her, drawing her up to his sleekly muscled body while his mouth moved with increasing urgency over hers until she suddenly surrendered to the hammering insistence of her own slowly awaking response. Like a symphony, his hands touched her body lightly in concert with the mounting demands of his mouth, drawing from her drugged senses a knowledge that her purpose in living was to bring happiness and fulfilment to this man above all others.

'I think it's time to begin your education,' he muttered thickly against her throat a moment later, and she saw nothing but the outline of his head against the outside darkness, the deep burning light in his eyes, as he bent swiftly to pick her up and carry her through the open balcony doors and across the sitting room to the bedroom with its wide canopied bed.

Jinny lay listening to the sound of Bret's electric shaver issuing from the spacious bathroom adjoining the bedroom, her lips curving into a slow smile of wonder at the implied intimacy in the open bathroom door. Drowsy contentment enveloped her when she remembered Bret's warm body beside hers in the night, his gentleness even when his own passion sought to control his actions, the depth of tenderness she had not suspected in the man he had become.

The shaver stopped, and Jinny heard a soft, tuneless whistle from the bathroom. Bret must surely be happy too! Suddenly she wanted to whistle herself, to dance, to whirl across the room into the arms of her husband. And why not? The reason for having a honeymoon was for two people to adjust to living together in the closest relationship there could ever be.

She threw back the covers and jumped from the wide bed to run across to the dressing table, picking up a comb there to draw it quickly through the dark tangle of curls round her face. Her hand was suddenly suspended in mid-air when she caught sight of the image reflected back to her in the bevelled mirror. There stood the Jinny she had always been, yet with a subtle difference in the soft luminous blue of her eyes, a new and more knowingly tender shape to her lips. She started when Bret spoke teasingly from the doorway.

'You look just the same, only more so.'

Jinny whirled to face him, gasping in dismay when she saw that he was already dressed in a dark business suit and pale blue shirt.

'Oh!' she explained in a voice of childish disappointment. 'You're going out.'

He came across the room and slid his arms round her waist, drawing her to him with a possessive movement that would have thrilled her had she not been preoccupied with the thought of his leaving her for business the morning after their wedding.

'Not because I want to, my darling,' he murmured close to her ear, then gently nuzzled the soft flesh beneath it.

'Then why go?' she asked breathily, her own mouth forming kisses along his jaw until she felt his body tense and his head rise sharply from her neck.

'Because—it's important to our future, yours and mine,' he told her unsteadily, his eyes going to the provocative fullness of her lips, swollen from his lovemaking. His mouth descended until she felt his breath warm on her face, and disappointment was released in a gasp when his fingers flexed suddenly against her spine, then lifted to her shoulders, pushing her away until she could see the struggle for control in his green-flecked grey eyes.

'If I kiss you now,' he muttered stiffly, 'I won't be able to leave you—and I must.'

He withdrew his hands from her shoulders and turned away, adding in a more normal tone: 'I've phoned down for breakfast. It should be here any minute, so don't bother about getting dressed first. You'll have plenty of time to do that while I'm out.'

'Are you—will you be gone for long?' Jinny asked hesitantly, sensing that this new husband of hers, however much he desired her as a woman, would not appreciate being quizzed about his movements.

'I'll be back in time to take you to Grouse Mountain for lunch,' he said placatingly. 'On a day like this, you can see for ever up there.'

Feeling happier because he had at least thought beyond the business affairs which would occupy his morning, Jinny showered quickly and donned the lace negligée matching her nightdress, knowing that its whiteness emphasised the darkness of her hair and cast a flattering glow upwards over her face. Her lips needed no addition of lipstick to enhance their natural cherry shade, and Bret whistled lightly when she came diffidently to sit opposite him at the portable table the waiter had placed by the balcony doors.

'Do you always look this good in the morning?' he asked with a pleased grin, coming round to pull out her chair and drop a kiss on the nape of her neck as she sat down. 'Mmm . . . you smell nice, too. I can see I'll have a hard time leaving you to tend to the cows every morning!'

'Harder than leaving me for plane business?' she couldn't resist asking with an upward tilt of her eyebrows, and wished immediately that she had left the words unsaid. His own brows dropped to a forbidding frown over suddenly glacial eyes as he moved back to his own place at the table and picked up the morning newspaper lying beside his plate.

'I've already explained about that,' he said curtly, and her eyes slid away from his seeming absorption in the newspaper to the television screen behind his broad shoulder. He had turned the volume so low that the newscaster's words were a mere murmur in the background, and Jinny watched uninterestedly as pictures of a revolutionary coup in a remote part of the world were flashed on the screen.

Would Bret be satisfied with the day-to-day running of the ranch, the details of which might seem humdrum to a man used to the thrust and parry of the business world? Would her own pleasure in making her home in the place she loved with the man she loved be offset by his increasing impatience to be back in the thick of things?

Lost in her thoughts, Jinny was reluctant to pull her attention back to what the television announcer was saying, although his words seared into her brain with devastating import.

'... in Seattle, renowned racing driver Eddie Clark was killed last night when he swerved to avoid another driver in difficulties. The freak accident ...'

'Bret?' Jinny was scarcely aware that she had spoken his name, but Bret's head had already swivelled round to the television set, the newspaper falling from his hand as he watched with horror scenes of the accident filling the screen. Then, suddenly animated into action, he came round to Jinny in two strides and held her face against the smooth silk of his shirt.

'Don't look, honey ... my God, Lesli! ...'

As if in answer to his shocked words, the announcer's suave tones went on to say that Eddie Clark's wife, when contacted at the Downshore Hotel, had refused to see reporters.

News coverage moved on to other less important matters and Bret went stiffly across the room to switch off the set.

Jinny sat where she was, her face frozen into an expression of stunned disbelief. Eddie killed ... Eddie dead ... her only memory of him was of a brown-haired young man with a devastating smile, the one who had taken Lesli away from Bret with hardly a backward glance. And Lesli—widowed after only seven years of marriage to the man she had fallen so deeply in love with that she had given up Bret.

'Jinny?'

Bret was bending over her and she shook her head to clear it before looking up into his awestruck eyes. As always when shock clouded her mind, she was more than ordinarily aware of the small things about him, the faint scent of aftershave cologne clinging to his skin, the deepened lines running between nose and mouth and round his eyes, the crisp set of his well-brushed hair.

'I'm going to phone Lesli,' he said, his voice deepened with emotion. 'She may need help. Did Eddie have any family?'

Jinny shook her head again. 'No—no, I don't think so.'

'Then I'll have to offer to go down there and help her.'

'I'll—come with you.'

'No,' he said decisively, straightening and looking grim. 'You've been through enough in that line lately. Do you want to talk to Lesli if I get through?'

She shrugged helplessly. 'I wouldn't know what to say ... after so long ... and now this.'

'All right.' His hand tightened on her shoulder momentarily before he turned away to the telephone on the desk. Its pale pink colour seemed incongruous against his bronzed hand and Jinny averted her eyes, staring instead across the balcony to the clearly etched mountains rising like sentinels behind the towers and rooftops. Bret's voice came as a low murmur from behind her, and she tried to project herself to the other end of the line to where Lesli was listening to that voice.

It had never been hard to picture her vivacious sister as

the adored wife of a well-known man, to know that she enjoyed every minute of travelling from place to place, country to country, meeting important people in all spheres of life. But Lesli a widow at twenty-eight was another matter. Could any other man ever fill Eddie's shoes for her?

'... don't worry, I'll be on my way as soon as I can get clearance,' Bret was saying huskily into the mouthpiece, adding a few more words in an even lower tone so that Jinny didn't catch them. She turned to glance across the room at him, and saw that although he had replaced the receiver his hand was still on it, his eyes holding a faraway look as he stared into space.

'Bret?'

He started and turned his head to look at her with a remoteness that brought a clutch of fear to her stomach. It was as if he had forgotten her existence.

'Sorry, Jinny, I was just wondering what would be the best thing to do about you. Lesli sounds all right, but I have the feeling she's pretty shocked underneath—which isn't surprising, poor kid.' His brow wrinkled in thought as he came across to the table, but he remained standing behind his chair. 'The thing is, I may be gone for a few days, Jinny. It might be better if I get Tom to take you back to the ranch and——'

'No!' she cried vehemently, jumping up and coming round to put a hand on his sleeve. 'Let me come with you, Bret. Lesli——'

'Lesli agrees with me it's best you don't come,' he stated flatly, seeming not to notice that her hand fell from his arm as he moved away, glancing at his watch. 'I have to cancel my business appointment for this morning. I'm already half an hour late for it.'

She watched numbly as he jabbed with an impatient finger on the telephone, then spoke to a man called Max, explaining the circumstances for the cancellation. Forlornly, she reflected that he had not found it necessary to forgo his meeting for the sake of their honeymoon, but for Lesli...

Honeymoon ... Tears stung the back of Jinny's eyes as disappointment surged through her. The beach cottage Bret had arranged was vacant for only the week of their honeymoon; for the rest of the summer, the family would be using it.

'Bret, don't go!' Impulsively, she half ran across the room to clutch at the hand which had already lifted the receiver again to call the airport. Bret's brows lifted in astonishment as the phone fell back with a clatter to its rest. 'We haven't even had our honeymoon yet! There must be lots of people down there willing to help Lesli ... she'll manage...'

'As I had to without her help when Pop died' trembled unsaid on her lips when she saw disbelief change to unwilling contempt in his eyes.

'I don't believe this,' he said with an impatient shake of his head, his eyes a cool grey as they appraised her uplifted face. 'Your sister has just been widowed in a particularly shocking way, yet all you can think of is a *honeymoon*?' His emphasis on the last word made it abundantly clear that in these circumstances he considered a honeymoon to be at the very bottom of his list of priorities, and that she was behaving like a child deprived of a useless toy. That he likened her to a child was evident in his next curtly spoken words. 'I'll arrange for you to be taken back to the ranch as soon as possible.'

The temper Jinny had almost forgotten she possessed flared up suddenly and she took a step back from him, her cheeks a flaming red. To be disposed of in the least bothersome way like an unwanted package was far from what she expected of her husband of only one day.

'No! If you won't take me with you, I'll stay right here till you get back,' she insisted stubbornly, unconsciously reinforcing his unspoken concept of her by thrusting out a rebellious lower lip.

'For God's sake, Jinny, I'm not going on a pleasure trip!'

'Aren't you?' she flashed back, seeing a quality of surprise and something else she could not at that moment define flicker in his eyes.

'Just what do you mean by that?' he asked with ominous quietness, reaching out with rapier swiftness to grasp her arm as she turned away, pulling her body unceremoniously against the unyielding stiffness of his taut muscles. Her eyes, darkened to an emotional dark blue, dropped away from the blazing anger in his.

'You never were indifferent to Lesli, were you?' she challenged in a small voice that made his grip relax suddenly on her arm so that she was free to move away several paces from him.

'No,' he returned evenly after a moment of chill silence. 'Lesli was never the kind a man could be indifferent to—he could either love her or hate her, there was no in between.' He sighed exasperatedly. 'But that was a long time ago. It has nothing to do with my reasons for going down there now.'

'Hasn't it?' she asked, fear putting a waspish note into her voice, though she hated displaying that fear to Bret, who she knew instinctively was the type of man to despise petty female jealousies.

'You can ask me that?—after last night?'

The trace of hurt in his grey eyes was overshadowed by the angry whiteness of his jaw, the compressed line of his mouth as he stared at her as if seeing her for the first time.

'Bret, I——'

'You have a lot of growing up to do yet, Jinny,' he interrupted shortly, turning to reach for the telephone again. 'Maybe you can use the time while I'm away to do some thinking.'

She was dismissed from his thoughts as he made arrangements for his flight to Seattle, standing with his well-set back to her while he issued instructions in a staccato voice to an employee named Dave. He did little more than glance Jinny's way with hard eyes when he passed her moments later to go into the bedroom, and she turned away with a sick feeling in the pit of her stomach. The balcony door slid back at a touch of her fingers and she stumbled across to the broad parapet at its outer edge, clutching the sun-warmed brick with trembling hands.

Far below, cars moved like busy ants along the wide street, miniature pedestrians sauntering with unhurried steps along the sidewalks reminding her that today was Saturday, less than twenty-four hours since the businesslike civil ceremony which had united her in marriage with Bret. Already there was a coolness between them, a rift that could only grow wider if he left to go to Lesli now. Her breath caught as a sob in her throat as she turned blindly back to the open doors and saw Bret, a valise in his hand, walking from the bedroom.

'Bret?—please don't go.'

He halted in mid-stride, and in the few seconds before he turned his head to look at her she felt an overwhelming longing to creep into his arms and be cradled against his broad chest like the child he thought her. The sudden rush of feeling sputtered and died in her breast when his eyes met the mute appeal in hers. His were the drab, remote grey of the Valley mountains before a storm came, eyes that sensed none of the anguish sweeping through her slender frame.

'I've made a commitment,' he said through stiff lips. 'I have to carry it through. I'll be back as soon as——'

'I love you, Bret,' she said tearfully, emotion lifting her voice to a higher key as she crossed the floor to stand before him, the negligée swishing against her legs as she walked.

Bret looked down quizzically into her upturned face and

shook his head slightly. 'I don't think you know the meaning of the word, Jinny—yet. One day you'll know that it involves trust—and loyalty—a host of things I haven't time to go into now.'

His cool lips touched her cheek briefly, and then he was gone with a suddenness that left Jinny frozen to the spot for long moments after the door had closed behind his dark-suited figure.

CHAPTER SIX

JINNY woke as the insistent ring sounded close to her ear, reaching out blindly to pick up the pink telephone from the desk next to the couch where she had inexplicably fallen asleep.

'Jinny? Is that you?'

Even through the blur of sleep Jinny recognised the breathlessly hurried voice of Karen, Bret's secretary and wife of his chief pilot Tom Roberts, both of whom had been the sole witnesses at the wedding the day before. Karen had the blonde good looks Jinny had selected for Bret's perfect woman, but it took only a few minutes in her company for Jinny to realise that Karen had eyes for no one but her equally fair husband, Tom.

'Yes,' she answered Karen's question dazedly. 'I'm afraid I fell asleep.'

'That's understandable,' Karen chuckled, then sobered quickly. 'I'm awfully sorry about your sister's husband, Jinny. It must have been a terrific shock for you, especially now when——'

'How did you know?'

'Well, Bret phoned Tom from the airport a while ago and asked us to keep an eye on you while he's gone.'

'Oh.'

'We'd love to have you come to dinner tonight,' Karen went on. 'Will it be all right if Tom picks you up around seven?'

Jinny demurred at first, then gave in to Karen's exuberant pleadings to join them, and sat staring at the phone for long minutes after she had rung off. Bret had been anxious enough about her to make arrangements for her to be taken care of at least part of the time he would be away. Or had he thought his good friends would have considered it odd if he had not done so?

She was ready and waiting in a simple sheath dress of midnight blue which blended perfectly with her eyes when Tom knocked on the suite door a little after seven.

'Wow!' he said, adding an appreciative whistle as his light blue eyes went over the dress that clung to her figure and outlined her every curve. 'No wonder Bret asked me to keep an eye on you!'

'Oh, I don't think Bret's the jealous type,' Jinny returned lightly as she lifted her white wool stole from a chair near the door.

Tom chuckled. 'Don't you believe it! Any man who's just married a beautiful girl wants to keep her all to himself —for a while, anyway.'

He kept up a voluble conversation as they descended in the elevator to where his car was parked far beneath the hotel, reminiscing about Eddie Clark's triumphs as a racing driver while Jinny's mind strayed back to his first words of greeting.

If Bret had truly loved her, would he have gone off so speedily to the aid of a woman who had dominated his love life for several years, even though it had all happened a long time ago? Was Lesli the reason Bret had never married, preferring instead relationships that were tenuous and unbinding? Most important of all, would he have married her, Jinny, if he had known that Lesli would be free, however tragically, so soon?

These and other questions occupied her mind as they sped through the thinning traffic to the ultra-modern house Tom and Karen had bought not far from the airport. Karen, in a black slim-fitting dress which emphasised her fairness, met them in the cedar-lined high-ceilinged hall and led Jinny into a living room furnished sparsely in the Scandinavian style. Although the surroundings were far from those Jinny would have chosen for herself, the modernistic background seemed to suit the vivid personalities of its owners, and she relaxed under their light-hearted bantering between themselves and the drinks Tom poured with a liberal hand. Strangely, Jinny felt herself to be Bret's wife far more here than she had until now. Their frequent references to him, taking for granted her interest in hearing about his exploits, gradually built up her confidence in herself as the wife of a man they both clearly loved and respected.

'I remember once,' Tom reminisced with a glint in his eye as they finished the superbly cooked meal, 'when a child up north needed drugs badly, and no one but Bret would take the risk of getting there and landing in such foul weather. He did it, though, by the skin of his teeth and the cost of a new set of landing skis—but the little girl lived, and Bret's more welcome there now than the flowers in May. And then there was the time when . . .'

Jinny listened, fascinated, as a side of her husband emerged which she had not even guessed at, and when she helped Karen with the dishes a short time later it was only to hear more of his praises sung.

'Bret's a wonderful guy—but then I don't have to tell *you* that! He's done so much for Tom and me in so many ways, I couldn't begin to tell you anyway. Well, look at the way he's left his day-old bride to go help her sister when he doesn't even know her!'

'Bret—knew my sister very well before her marriage,' Jinny got out with difficulty, remembrance rushing over her with Karen's admiringly spoken words. 'They were—almost engaged.'

Karen's head swivelled round from the dishwasher where she was stacking the dishes, the unspoken heartache behind Jinny's soft utterance bringing a thoughtful look to her light blue eyes.

'If you're thinking what I think you're thinking,' she said with clear deliberation, 'you have it all wrong. Bret's the most honest, sincere man I know apart from Tom, and I know him pretty well, having worked for him almost since the beginning of Stafford Air-North. Look, Jinny,' she added, turning back to close the dishwasher, 'let's you and me have a little talk while the dishes are doing. Tom's watching baseball on television, so he won't miss us.'

Jinny moved obediently to the dinette table Karen waved to, and shortly the fair girl came to sit opposite her while the dishwasher churned quietly in the background. Declining with a shake of her head the cigarette Karen offered her, Jinny watched while the other girl lit up and inhaled deeply before looking directly across the table.

'I don't think it's telling tales out of school to say that I've seen Bret with quite a few women since I've been working for him. He's a very attractive man, as you obviously know, and I don't believe it's exaggerating to say he'd only have to crook a finger to have his world filled with beautiful women.' Karen paused and stared for a moment at the red glow on her cigarette's tip.

'That's why I—well, frankly, when he told me he was going to marry a girl from the middle of nowhere I was sceptical, to say the least. It just didn't seem Bret's style to marry a simple country girl.' She sighed, then smiled into Jinny's apprehensive eyes. 'But when I saw you together, saw the way Bret looked at you—well, I'd never seen him look at any other woman that way, and I knew you were right for him. Flying is in Bret's blood just as much as it is in Tom's, and I can't imagine Tom giving it up for my sake as Bret's doing for you.'

'It isn't for me exactly,' Jinny protested uncomfortably. 'Bret's first love was ranching, long before he ever thought of planes and flying. Besides, he's not giving up flying completely. The company is still his, and he has a plane at the ranch.'

'What made him give up ranching if he loved it so much?' Karen asked curiously. 'As I understood it, he was the only son of a prosperous rancher and could have——'

'He—left Gold Valley when Lesli, my sister, eloped with Eddie Clark,' Jinny interrupted jerkily.

'Oh. I see.' Karen's brow wrinkled as she looked across into Jinny's vulnerable eyes. 'Still, I'm positive Bret Stafford would never marry one girl while still holding a torch for another. It would be completely out of character for him to do that. You'll find he'll come back just as loving as ever after doing the necessary for your sister.' Her smile was faintly sardonic. 'It's that Sir Galahad streak in his nature that made him leave you in the first place, not because he's still infatuated with your sister, so cheer up, honey. He's more than worth waiting for.'

'Yes ... yes, he is,' Jinny agreed with a sudden breathless smile, her heart swelling with renewed confidence under Karen's kindly concern. 'Thanks, Karen. I guess I was just being silly.'

She left just before ten, anxious in case Bret should phone the hotel and find her out, but there was no call from him that night, nor the next. Nevertheless, her high mood of confidence stayed with her, giving an inner glow to her eyes and a smile to her lips which brought half envious looks from passersby in the park where she walked for long hours during the day.

Bret had more than enough to do, she told herself under the shower on the second night, seeing to all the inevitable details of Eddie's death for Lesli, without placing long-

distance calls to the bride who had sent him away a disappointed man. He had made no promises about calling
her, probably assuming her evenings would be spent with
Karen and Tom.

As the warm water ran caressingly over the curves and
indentations of her body, sparking memories of Bret's
skilled hands awakening an earthshaking response she
would hardly have dreamed possible, she knew she had not
disappointed him physically. It was in the other areas,
which she was just beginning to realise were equally important in a successful marriage, that she had let him down.
What had he said? 'Trust' and 'loyalty' were the two
qualities he had particularly mentioned, neither of which
she had displayed that morning. Shame washed over her
when she reflected that his secretary, Karen, had had far
more faith in his integrity than she herself had.

Jinny climbed into the wide bridal bed and switched off
the bedside lamp, watching abstractedly the play of light
from outside on the ceiling. Maybe this separation so soon
in their marriage had been necessary for her to learn a
valuable lesson which might never have been learned other-
wise. Happily, it wasn't too late to set their feet in the right
direction after a false start.

Not long after she fell asleep smiling in anticipation of
Bret's delighted surprise at her newly-won maturity. 'I did
what you said to do, Bret darling,' she would say. 'I did a
lot of thinking while you were gone, and ...'

It was evening of the next day when the pink telephone
buzzed discreetly just as Jinny sat down at the portable
table the room service waiter had wheeled in. Excitement
coursed through her as she rushed across the room, almost
making her drop the receiver as she raised it to her ear and
said breathlessly: 'Bret?'

'No, it's Tom, Jinny,' the male voice said awkwardly,
seeming embarrassed. 'But I'm calling for Bret. He just

phoned from Seattle and asked me to let you know that he'll be back around six-thirty tomorrow evening.'

'Oh.' Disappointment at not hearing Bret's voice rose to form a lump in her throat, constricting her vocal chords.

'He sounded in a big hurry, Jinny,' Tom excused. 'I guess that's why he didn't call you direct. We have to make landing arrangements at this end, so——'

'It's all right, Tom, I understand,' she got out after swallowing the lump. 'I didn't expect him to call both of us. Thanks for letting me know.'

Tears battled with common sense as she walked slowly back to the table and took her place before the tenderloin beef slices smothered with mushrooms in a cream sauce and flanked by a colourful salad. In the same automatic way, her hand lifted the fork and began to move the salad from place to place on the plate until suddenly common sense lost the battle and tears forced themselves from her eyes and ran down her cheeks.

The fork dropped with a clatter on the oval plate when she pushed back her chair blindly and fled to the sofa, curling up with her head on her arm while the tears fell unchecked. Only now, when she knew with certainty that Bret would not be phoning her, did she realise how much she had longed for the comfort of his voice telling her that he was sorry they had parted on bad terms, that he missed her as much as she could possibly miss him, that all would be well when he held her in his arms again.

At last she raised her head, groping for her handkerchief and blowing her nose furiously when she found it. Of course Bret hadn't wanted to phone her. He was unaware of her changed, more mature emotions, and had probably decided, harrowed as the past few days must have left him, to leave well enough alone until they met face to face. Buoyed with this conviction, Jinny rose and approached the beef slices with a more appreciative eye, and the waiter later nodded his approval at the small amount she left on the plate.

'You are recovering your appetite, madam,' he said in his soft Italian accent as he stacked the used dishes neatly and almost noiselessly.

'Yes—my husband's coming back tomorrow,' Jinny confided with a starry smile to the romantically inclined older man whose liquid eyes had expressed his deep compassion for a bride parted so precipitately from her new husband.

'Ah, *bene*, *bene*,' he beamed, and Jinny watched him wheel the trolley away, gratitude filling her eyes. She must tell Bret how kind the hotel staff had been, from the manager who had come in person to express his regrets down to the maid who kept the bridal suite in its romantically inspiring state with fresh flowers daily, even though Jinny was the only occupant.

The taxi dropped her off just before six-thirty at the entrance to the Stafford Air-North hangar, and when Jinny had paid him off she looked with awed interest round the large echoing space where planes of various sizes were interspersed across the dark grey concrete floor. Until this moment, the charter business Bret had built up from one plane had been words meaning little to her. Now, as evidence of his enterprise and business acumen stretched before her like a vast aerial empire, awe deepened to unbelievable gladness that such a man had chosen her for his wife.

Her slow steps halted when a tinkling noise of metal on metal drifted across the cavernous hangar. She had expected that the employees would have gone home long before now, but perhaps one had remained to take care of Bret's plane when he arrived.

Threading her way between the gleaming white and red planes, she came across a young mechanic crouched under the dust-smeared body of a four-seater Cessna, his fair-skinned face generously smudged with dark oil. He jumped up when Jinny approached, rubbing his face with a grubby-

looking cloth as he came towards her with appraising eyes
that took in every detail of her carefully chosen dark blue
skirt suit and slender legs given a sleek line with high-
heeled navy sandals. Admiration sparked in his pale blue
eyes as he said:

'Can I help you, miss?'

'Yes, I—where's the best place to wait for Mr Stafford's
arrival?'

'He came in a few minutes ago in this baby,' he grinned,
jerking a thumb behind him to the Cessna. 'He's still in the
office, I think, over there.' The boy pointed to one side of
the hangar where glass-fronted offices overlooked the work
area. 'His office is on the right along that passage in the
middle—but I wouldn't go in there right now if I was you,'
he called after Jinny's retreating figure. 'He's busy
with——'

'It's all right,' she turned to smile, 'he's my husband.'

She caught a glimpse of his startled jaw-drop as she went
lightly towards the office block, and a smile still curved the
corner of her mouth when she entered the small passage in
search of Bret's office.

Fingers of excitement curled softly in her stomach at the
thought of seeing his tall figure, of being held in his arms
again. Strange that his face should have become a jumbled
blur in her mind, but hadn't she read somewhere that it was
easier to remember the features of a casual acquaintance
than those of someone deeply loved?

Glass walls exposed the offices on either side of the passage, but Jinny's eyes were directed to the right where a
nameplate halfway along read 'Bret Stafford, President'. A
sharp pang of disappointment shot through her when she
saw the deserted office. She had missed Bret after all!

Further inspection through the glass revealed that the
office was more that of a secretary's than the head of the
firm's, and her eyes had barely focused on an open door on
the far wall when a desk lamp was switched on and she saw

Bret's figure clearly outlined in front of the desk. Almost before recognition registered, Jinny felt weak at the knees and wondered how she could have thought his features lost to her. Piercingly familiar was the set of his broadly confident shoulders, the profile of proudly straight nose and firmly chiselled lips over a decisively set chin. He appeared to be listening to someone out of Jinny's sight and she watched, mesmerised, as his arms lifted and opened to receive a slim black-clad figure, his cheek coming down after a moment's hesitation to rest against the light brown head which fitted into his shoulder as if well used to being there.

Nausea rose up to almost choke Jinny with its bitterness. Lesli! Bret had brought Lesli back with him! Distorted pictures of them in each other's arms for the past four days crowded for space in Jinny's reeling mind, yet she stood transfixed, longing to run away while at the same time hypnotised into watching the silent figures cling together as if carved of stone. Her own head lifted when Lesli's rose slightly from Bret's shoulder and traced soft kisses along his jawline, stopping only when his hands unclasped from her waist and dug whitely into her upper arms as he pulled back to say something.

What was he saying! 'Let's wait, my darling, until I'm free of Jinny. She's such a child, she doesn't know the meaning of love as we do, as we always have.'

As if Bret had actually shouted those words inches from her ears, Jinny stumbled blindly back along the passage hearing their booming reverberation in her brain. Pain rose in sick waves from the pit of her stomach and made her seek refuge in a deep niche at the end of the passage, and she leaned her forehead against the rough coolness of the bricks as dry sobs shook her without giving the blessed relief of tears.

Another voice echoed in the numbed recesses of her mind while she shivered in the corner like a wounded animal. 'Lesli will always get what she wants without raising a

finger,' her grandfather had once said—'but you, my darlin'
—you'll have to be hurt badly before you learn to fight for
what's yours.'

Jinny's head lifted, her breath catching in her throat.
Fight! If only she could fight Lesli on her own terms ...
but how impossible that was had been demonstrated a few
moments before. Jinny knew she was no match for a widow
of days who could stir passionate ardour in a man she had
not seen for seven years—that man, moreover, having just
married her younger sister. Legally Bret was Jinny's, but
what did legality matter when his heart lay elsewhere?

A feeling of revulsion swept over her and left her shaken.
The love for Bret that had been part of her very being from
girlhood broke slowly into a thousand pieces inside her,
reassembling to form an icy core of hatred for the man who
had lifted her to heights she had not known existed, then
cast her down as far the other way.

Cool plans began to form in her mind as she straightened
away from the wall. No doubt Bret and Lesli were making
plans of their own for their future together, but she, Jinny,
held the trump card. In the eyes of the law, Bret was hers,
and she meant to keep it that way as long as possible ...

Jinny stepped out of the niche and was almost bowled over
by a hurrying figure entering the passage.

'Jinny!' Tom exclaimed as his arm went round her to
steady her. 'I'm sorry, are you hurt?'

She shook her head and smiled into his concerned face.
'No, I'm fine, Tom. Did you come to see Bret too?'

'If I'm not too late. Doug tells me his plane got in half
an hour early.'

'I think he's still there.' Jinny started to walk towards
Bret's office. 'I wasn't sure where I'd find him.'

'Oh, of course, you haven't been in the hangar before,
have you? It's right down here.'

Tom took her arm and chatted companionably while they

went past the glass windows, and Jinny saw Bret emerge from the inner office behind the sleekly glamorous Lesli. Tom saw them at the same time and seemed embarrassed as he stepped in front of Jinny, obscuring her view of the couple inside.

'Bret seems to be busy with a client right now—maybe we should wait in the hangar.'

Jinny smiled with false sunniness. 'It's all right, Tom. She's my sister.'

'Oh!' said Tom, evidently relieved as he opened the door into the office.

Bret nodded briefly to Tom, but his eyes reached beyond to where Jinny stood, the smile still fixed on her face. The smile changed to one of sardonic amusement when he stepped forward and injected a note of eager welcome into his voice.

'Jinny! I'm glad you came down to the airport. I——'

'So this is Jinny? My little sister?' Lesli interrupted from his side, her voice grown more husky with the years though nothing else seemed to have changed. Her eyes were still the sparkling amber colour Jinny remembered, her small straight nose and fully curved lips as attractive as ever. She held out black-clad arms dramatically, and Jinny walked past Bret to be enfolded in them.

'Darling. I'd never have known you!' Lesli exclaimed after offering Jinny a cool cheek to receive an equally cold kiss from her. 'You were just a funny little girl with black braids round your head when I last saw you. Why, you've grown into quite a pretty girl—hasn't she, Bret?'

'That's a charged question to ask *me*,' he returned shortly, seeming annoyed that Jinny had gone past him to greet her sister first.

'It certainly is,' Tom put in heartily, betraying his uneasy feeling of something going on beyond his understanding. 'All men are prejudiced when it comes to their brides.'

'Yes, of course,' Lesli agreed with silky smoothness, re-

taining the hold she had claimed on Jinny's waist while
Bret introduced Tom. 'I really feel so badly about coming
up here to interrupt their honeymoon, but Bret absolutely
insisted, didn't you, darling?'

'Yes,' he said tersely, his eyes puzzled as they rested on
Jinny's composed face beside Lesli's. 'You need time
to——'

'Bret's right,' Jinny interposed sweetly. 'I'm glad he
brought you back with him. You must stay at Gold Valley
for as long as you like.'

Both Bret and Lesli looked warily at her, and she felt a
hysterical desire to giggle. Probably neither of them had
anticipated such ready acquiescence to their plans.

They all moved slowly out of the office and along the
passage, Lesli holding Jinny's arm while she related in a
voice filled with pathos the details of Eddie's burial in a
small town not far from Seattle. '. . . strangely enough, this
little place was the only spot Eddie ever called home. He
was brought up by two maiden aunts there, both dead long
ago, of course . . .'

As Lesli prattled on Jinny felt only compassion for
Eddie, whose wife of seven years had consigned him to the
same oblivion as the maiden ladies who had nurtured him
in life and lay beside him in death.

Bret and Tom walked behind them discussing business,
but when they reached the low and darkly sleek company
car parked at the end of the passage Tom sprang forward to
hold the front passenger door open and Lesli installed herself there with no thought of Jinny behind her.

'There's room for three in the front,' said Bret, putting a
hand under Jinny's elbow to lead her to the other side of the
car.

'It's all right,' she said hurriedly without looking at him,
opening the rear door herself. 'I'll have to get used to the
back seat now, won't I?'

He held the door open with one hand and looked down

into her deceptively innocent eyes, a baffled frown forming between his own so that his brows winged upward in a puzzled arc. Then, his lips tightening to a hard line, he stepped back and slammed the door with more force than necessary, stopping to exchange a few more words with Tom before going round to thrust himself behind the wheel.

Lesli appeared not to notice the strained silence between them as they drove in the powerful car away from the hangar. Her animated monologue seemed to require no more than an occasional grunt from Bret, but Jinny was acutely conscious of his eyes fixed in puzzled speculation on her own image in the rear view mirror each time she glanced up. At last she averted her eyes from the front altogether and concentrated on the passing buildings. Traffic had grown light after the evening rush hour, and there were no delays as they swept over the bridge spanning the Fraser River into Vancouver.

The hotel doorman stepped forward to open the car doors for Lesli and Jinny, at the same time seeing Bret's almost imperceptible nod towards the car as he stepped out. Lifting a hand, the doorman summoned a uniformed boy, who came rushing forward to listen to Bret's quiet instructions before taking his place behind the wheel. As he drove the car off into the underground parking lot, Bret came between the two girls and took an elbow of each as they mounted the steps into the hotel.

'I'll see about getting you a room for tonight,' he said to Lesli when they reached the foyer, adding more stiffly to Jinny: 'I thought it might be better if we stay here over-night before going on to the ranch tomorrow.'

Lesli had turned away to look interestedly round the Carillon's foyer and Jinny said with a wide-eyed look: 'Oh? I thought we were all going on honeymoon together!' and felt Bret's fingers dig sharply into her tender flesh. 'We could still have a day or two at the beach cottage.'

'That sounds marvellous!' Lesli put in, having heard

only the mention of a beach cottage. 'I love the water.'

'The cottage isn't suitable for more than two,' Bret gritted through tightly drawn lips, dropping their arms abruptly. 'You'll find it peaceful enough at the ranch.'

Lesli frowned at his retreating back as he strode towards the reception desk. 'Jinny, my dear, we must point out a few of the disadvantages of living tucked away in the country,' she said with a heavy sigh.

'Why? I liked it there too.'

'Only because you've never known anywhere else,' Lesli rejoined loftily, her light brown eyes narrowing as they focused on Bret's back in an excellently tailored suit which made the most of his broad shoulders and tapered hips. 'I ask you, can you imagine a man like that wasting his talents on mangy old cows and cleaning out the stables?'

'Valley Ranch doesn't have mangy cows,' Jinny defended hotly. 'Stafford beef is as prime as you can get—and he has men to clean out the stables.'

Lesli's eyes turned with sharp amusement to meet hers. 'My, you *are* in love, aren't you? But then you always were, weren't you? With Bret, I mean. Even in the days when he was mad about me.' She gave a low chuckle of reminiscence. 'I can remember when he used to beg me to marry him, poor darling—he must have been really devastated when I ran off with Eddie, wasn't he?'

'Yes,' Jinny admitted honestly, though her finger nails cut into her palms as she clenched her hands.

'I've often wondered if I did the right thing, going off with Eddie that way,' her sister mused, her eyes going back to where Bret was turning away from the desk. 'But who could have known Bret would turn out to be the success he is? All he cared about in those days was that wretched Valley and ranches.'

'He still does,' Jinny said quietly, her heart turning over as she watched Bret's progress towards them. Even surrounded by other men of prepossessing appearance, he

stood out as a man of forceful distinction. That he had held
her in his arms and made love to her, Jinny O'Brien from a
remote township called Gold Valley, for even one brief
night, seemed incomprehensible to her.

'Ah, well, we'll have to see what we can do to change
that,' Lesli murmured, smiling down when Bret approached.

'I've got you a room on the fourth floor—408,' he said,
barely answering her smile, and Jinny averted her eyes
from the face that was only too familiar in its dearness.
Hatred had dissolved in her already. How could she go
through with the pretence that she cared nothing for him
when her knees turned to water whenever he came near?
Numbly she fell into step beside Lesli and walked to the
elevator.

Bret punched two buttons for their respective floors and
was silent until the elevator stopped at the fourth level.
Taking Lesli's arm, he said curtly to Jinny: 'I'll be up in a
few minutes,' and was disappearing with the elegant black-
clad figure down the carpeted corridor when the doors
closed again on Jinny's pinched face.

The bridal suite's obvious romantic overtones struck her
as too sweetly sentimental when she let herself in moments
later. The delicate pink rosebuds in vases everywhere
seemed to mock her as she walked through into the bedroom and went to stand before the dressing table, surveying
herself morosely in the mirror. The well-cut navy suit, fitting closely to her figure and emphasising the curves above
and below her small waist, was suddenly like a coat of mail
on her. Fiercely, she longed for the casual jeans and light
tops she had left behind at Gold Valley, the everyday
clothes she felt comfortable in.

She had already unbuttoned the jacket when a tap
sounded at the outer door and her fingers froze. Bret! He
would have to knock to get in because she had the key to the
suite. Panic swept over her in an icy flow, and she knew she

wasn't ready to face him yet without Lesli's intervening presence.

A second, sharper knock sent her trembling fingers to refasten the buttons, and she crossed the sitting room with pounding heart, feeling almost hysterical with relief when she found the young man who had driven the car away staring with bored eyes at the white-panelled door. At his feet lay Bret's travel bag.

'Oh, I'm sorry,' she gasped. 'I was just——'

'That's all right, ma'am,' he said laconically, picking up the bag and depositing it inside the door. 'We never expect a speedy reply from the bridal suite.'

Colour flooded Jinny's face, and to cover her embarrassment she offered to pay him for his trouble.

'No need, thanks. Mr Stafford saw to all that.'

He went out with a cheery grin, and Jinny re-fastened the door, her heart still pounding. What had happened to all the self-control, the coolness she had mustered at the airport after seeing Lesli in Bret's arms? All she knew at this moment was that she couldn't face Bret, knowing he would come reluctantly to her from Lesli's room. He had already been there for fifteen minutes, and she closed her eyes against the visions that arose before them of passionate love scenes being enacted on the fourth floor far below.

She ran across the sitting room, unbuttoning her jacket as she went. At least she would have a respite, a time to collect her scattered emotions, under the shower.

Ingrained neatness made her hang up her jacket and skirt in the closet before she rushed into the bathroom, feeling secure only when she had locked the door and could lean with closed eyes against it. Bret would be angry at having to go down and ask for an extra key to the suite when there was no answer to his knock—but maybe he would go back to join Lesli, making a joke of Jinny's childish refusal to open the door.

She stepped under the warm shower spray, thankful for

its insulation against other noises, and scarcely felt the tears
mingling with the gentle rivulets of water running down her
face. The soothing warmth relaxed her, and she had no idea
of how long she had been standing under the shower when
she at last turned off the taps and stepped out. Her hand
reached up to the hook behind the door after she had dried
herself, a frown of annoyance marking her brow as she remembered that she had moved her robe from there that
morning, tidying the suite for Bret's homecoming.

She bit her lip, then put one ear to the door panel. There
was no sound from the other rooms. Quickly wrapping a
dry towel round her, she opened the door cautiously and
padded across the carpet to the bedroom, coming to a gasping halt when Bret's grim-faced figure rose from the silk-
covered tub chair by the window.

'How—how did you get in?' she breathed, noticing in an
abstracted way that although he had loosened his tie and
unbuttoned his shirt halfway, he still wore the suit jacket.

'Fortunately I had the foresight to ask for an extra key at
the desk,' he said drily. His eyes flickered over her scantily
clad body, but he made no move towards her. 'Now maybe
you'll be good enough to explain what all this frigid business is about.'

'Er—frigid?'

'Frigid,' he confirmed flatly. 'Ever since Lesli and I got
back——'

'Oh, yes, Lesli,' she said softly, her eyes narrowing
slightly as she went towards the dressing table, but she had
taken only two steps when he reached out a hand and jerked
her round by the wrist to face him.

'So that's it! You're mad because I brought Lesli back,
aren't you? Good God, Jinny, she's your sister. She needs
your understanding right now, not your suspicions!'

'That's your reason for bringing her back here?—because
she needs *my* understanding?'

Traitorous hope surged in her breast that that was indeed

his reason for bring Lesli, that the scene she had witnessed at the airport was one of consolation more than passion, but the hope died an untimely death when his eyes dropped away from hers and he released her hand.

'It's not the only reason, no,' he admitted quietly. 'You've always known that I——'

'Oh, yes, Bret, I've always known,' she interrupted bitterly, controlling the note of hysteria in her voice as she went on: 'I didn't need to see that touching little scene at the airport to——'

'*What?*'

'I saw it, Bret, so there's no point in denying it.'

She defied her shoulders to droop as she went at last to sit at the dressing table, picking up the brush lying there and beginning to stroke her hair with it. The dark fronds still curled damply round her cheeks from the shower, and when the bristles swept through it they fluffed out, making her look much younger than her twenty-one years.

Perhaps that was what made Bret stride up behind her and say tautly: 'For God's sake, put that brush down and come here.'

The brush fell with a clatter on the glassed surface of the dressing table as he jerked her to her feet, his eyes searching hers with angry intensity before his head swooped and his mouth fastened fiercely on hers. His hands dug into the soft flesh of her bare shoulders, paining her so much that her lips parted under the relentless assault of his, her body responding mindlessly to his harsh ardour by straining up to meld into the damp warmth of his shirt front.

His hands slid over her smooth shoulders and contacted the confining folds of the thick towel, which he discarded as if it were a cotton rag and ran his hands over her silkily sensitive skin until she sagged against him. He pulled his mouth away from hers then and buried his face in her neck, murmuring the words she had longed to hear in her ear and pressing her head against his jacketed shoulder. As always when her emotions were at their highest peak, her nostrils picked up the warm scent of his skin, the faint pungency of cigar tobacco ... and something else which eluded identification.

A faint smile tinged his lips when the darkened blue of her eyes met the heavy-lidded grey-green of his momentarily before his head bent to kiss the soap-scented valley between her breasts. There was contentment in the smile, and a quality that was almost—triumphant! As that word burst like a shooting star into her consciousness, she knew at once the source of the scent on Bret's jacket—Lesli's perfume, its distinctive musky odour impossible to mistake.

He half staggered when Jinny dragged herself away from him and bent swiftly to pick up the discarded towel from their feet.

'What the——?'

'You really are very easily roused, aren't you, Bret?' she mocked, tucking in the loose end of the towel and padding barefoot to the closet. 'Does Lesli know that any available woman can turn you on?'

She slid open the closet door and selected blindly a full-length dress, a sheath in sparkling white, laying it on the bed before turning to glance at his silent figure, feeling a momentary pang when she saw that his face had turned to ashen grey, a shade that almost matched his eyes.

'If that's the way you feel, I can't see that there's any point in carrying on with this marriage,' he said in a lifeless, cracked voice. 'Mutual trust seems to be lacking on your part. I'll see my lawyer on Monday about an annulment.'

He turned to the door, but swung back incredulously when Jinny said vehemently: 'Oh, no, Bret! It's not going to be as easy as that!'

She took a step towards him, forgetting the scantiness of her attire in the blaze of anger that coursed through her. 'Isn't an annulment only granted when the marriage hasn't been—what do the lawyers call it?—consummated?'

Dark colour ran up under his skin, contrasting with the tense white line of his jaw. His eyes bored into hers across the room until she turned away and smoothed the uncreased dress on the bed.

'Am I to take it that you *want* to stay married to me in spite of——'

'Yes!' she ejaculated fiercely, facing him again. 'I mean to make it as difficult as possible for you and Lesli to get together—legally, anyway. You're married to me, for better or for worse, Bret, and that's the way it's going to stay until——'

'Until?' he prompted coldly when she paused.

'Until it suits me to let you go. Oh, don't worry,' she went on with a scornful lift to her voice, 'I'll cook for you, clean for you, and do everything a wife does except——' She broke off again and bit her lip.

He regarded her in bitter silence for long moments before saying icily: 'That can be grounds for divorce too, you know. But don't worry,' he went on when she gave him a look of surprise mingled with fear, 'I won't be insisting on my marital rights—I've never had to take a woman by force yet!'

This reminder of his attractiveness to other women registered as a shaft of pain rising to cut off the breath from her throat. Possessing women came as naturally as breathing to him. Perhaps Mike had not been too far off the mark after all when he had said that Bret would never be happy with one woman. If it hadn't been Lesli, there would have been someone else.

Where would he go tonight? To Lesli? Another room in the hotel? No, she decided immediately. He was too proud to want the hotel staff to speculate about his short-lived marriage. That same pride would prevent his seeking a divorce on the grounds he had mentioned, she was sure, but there was little triumph in her as she threw herself on the bed, rumpling the white dress as she gave vent to the tears she had been holding back with such great effort.

Bret was hers in every sense except the one most important to her ... How long could she keep up the pretence of theirs being a normal marriage? Particularly when Lesli, the woman he had always loved, was there at the ranch as a living bone of contention?

CHAPTER SEVEN

JINNY sighed and went to stare from the kitchen window while coffee for Lesli's breakfast tray percolated on the stove.

She had found it easier during their six weeks at Valley Ranch to take Lesli's breakfast to her around ten. That way, she had the hours between Bret's leaving and Lesli's appearance entirely to herself, hours which had become precious to her as a time when she could be herself with no part to play as a participant in a marriage that was no marriage.

The living areas had gradually become transformed during those hours when she could pretend that she was a normal, happy housewife. New slipcovers on the living-room furniture, brilliant poppies on a neutral background, had changed the sombre tones of the room to one of welcoming and gay comfort, while potted flowering plants lit the corners and windowsills. Even Bret had stood motionless in the doorway when it was done, unable to hide the approval in his grey eyes, though as he turned away he remarked in the cool voice he reserved for Jinny: 'There's still something missing ... but I don't suppose you've noticed that.'

Now as she leaned across the sink to see the patriotic red, white and blue of the petunias she had planted in a wide

band round the flagstone terrace, Jinny wondered again
what he had meant. Perhaps a picture or two on the walls to
replace the faded prints that had been there for untold years.
Nothing else remained to be done ... she had shampooed
the large areas of thick rug and polished the furniture until
it gleamed, and had even attacked the rough stone of the
fireplace to remove the traces of previous fires from its surface.

She woke from her reverie with a start, realising that the
coffee was ready to pour into the glass container on Lesli's
tray. In another two minutes she had lifted the tray, set
with a daintily formed cup and saucer and plate of crisp
rolls which with coffee was all Lesli had for breakfast, and
went along to the bedroom she had used herself on the day
of her dunking in the mud.

Daylight flooded the room when Jinny pulled back the
heavy curtains, and she saw that her sister's eyelids were
fluttering mutinously as she laid the tray on the bedside
table.

'Heavens, Jinny, must you make that awful racket? My
head's throbbing like a sledgehammer!' Lesli pulled herself
up against the pillows in one sensuous movement, the pale
tan of her low-cut nightdress the same colour as her skin.

'You shouldn't drink so much,' Jinny responded crisply,
pouring coffee into the china cup and handing it unceremoniously to her sister.

Even in the disadvantageous light of waking from sleep,
Lesli was beautiful with her light brown hair tumbling
round her face to her shoulders, her amber eyes fringed
with darker lashes, her mouth a soft provocative bow. No
wonder Bret—Jinny checked the thought that had arisen in
her mind more than once since they had set up this *ménage
à trois* on their return from Vancouver.

Not that she had witnessed any more love scenes between
them since their return ... there had scarcely been an
opportunity for them to be alone. Bret always rose when she

did at bedtime, walking along the passage with her as if they shared the large master bedroom, but after a tersely formal 'Goodnight' he would leave her to go to his office next door. Half of the wood-panelled office held a big-topped desk of walnut and businesslike furniture while the other half was furnished as a single bedroom from the days of his mother's last illness.

'Who wouldn't drink a lot when Bret insists on asking all those dreary people over almost every night?' Lesli now complained, drinking thirstily from her cup. 'I swear I'll scream if one more rustic mother figure sheds tears over Eddie again!'

'They mean well,' Jinny said sharply. 'Losing a husband is the worst thing they can imagine happening to a woman.'

'Well, it wasn't the worst thing that happened to me!' Lesli snapped. 'Eddie and I had been going our own ways for a long time before the crash—why do you think I wasn't at the track the day he was killed? No, darling, I was having a wonderful time with Jacques Fournier ... luckily his car developed some kind of trouble that kept him out of the race.'

Jinny stared with mounting horror at her sister's beautiful face. 'Did Eddie know that you were—with this man?'

'Of course he did!' Lesli waved a hand impatiently. 'Oh, he put on his great act of being the jealous husband before he left for the track, but I'd grown used to that. He was always insanely jealous of any man I looked at twice. I can tell you it's very wearing to live with someone like that.' Her yellow-brown eyes narrowed slightly as she looked up at Jinny. 'But that's a problem you don't have, isn't it?'

Jinny's mouth felt suddenly dry. 'What do you mean?'

'Oh, come on, darling,' Lesli laughed softly without mirth. 'I know you've been in love with Bret for years, even when he was begging me to marry him, but a blind man wouldn't be deceived into thinking he returns your adoration. I must say, it's a puzzle to me why he married you at all—not that you aren't pretty and fairly intelligent,' she added with a perfunctory smile, '—but I'm sure you'd be the first to admit that you're hardly the type for a man like Bret. He needs someone bright and vivacious, someone who can get him over this passing phase of wanting to be a rancher.'

'Someone like you, you mean?' Jinny asked tightly.

'Well—yes.' Lesli looked up speculatively at her through the veil of her lashes, then said huskily: 'You must know that when two people were as close as Bret and I were at one time, something always remains of that feeling.' She paused before going on in a confidingly reminiscent manner: 'As soon as I heard his voice on the phone, I knew nothing had changed between us. And I could tell that when he saw me he felt exactly the same ... poor Bret, can you imagine how he felt, realising that and knowing he had rushed into marriage with you because he was sorry for you after Pop died, and——'

'I thought you said it was a puzzle to you why he married me at all?' Jinny asked, her voice grown cold and hard. She had been right in sensing that, for reasons of his own, Bret had not confided in Lesli the outcome of his quarrel with Jinny the night of their arrival in Vancouver. The thought gave her a bleak kind of pleasure. At least he had enough decency to finish with one unwanted woman before taking up with the one he desired as his wife.

'I can't help feeling there was a little more to it than that,' Lesli went on in answer to Jinny's question, her smoothly tanned brow wrinkling in concentration as she turned to pour more coffee into her cup. It was as if they were discussing the reasons for a merger between two companies, no feelings involved.

'Maybe he married me for the gold on Hillside Ranch!' Jinny retorted sarcastically as she moved towards the door.

'Gold? What gold?'

Jinny laughed shortly. 'The gold Pop always dreamed

was there. But you can discount that as Bret's reason for marrying me—he doesn't believe it exists.'

Lesli looked suddenly thoughtful as Jinny went out, and brought up the subject of gold at the dinner table that night when the three of them sat down to the meal Jinny had cooked. Roasting the leg of lamb in the sun-drenched kitchen had brought a light flush to her cheeks, a pink that matched the roses on her sleeveless floral dress.

'Bret, what would the chances be of finding gold in this area?' Lesli asked with the deferential air of one seeking superior knowledge.

Bret, his hair still showing damp from the shower he had taken on coming in from the calf pens, looked piercingly across the oval table at Jinny and said with deliberate slowness: 'If you mean at Hillside Ranch, none at all. The seams were all worked out long ago, and I'm glad of it. Mines and cattle don't blend too well together.'

'Pop had faith in finding gold at Hillside,' Jinny threw back with stubborn heat. 'And I'd rather believe him than——'

The unspoken 'you' hung over the table between them, and Bret's jaw tightened ominously, though he said no more. Lesli dropped the subject, turning instead to the idea she had had during the afternoon while sunning herself on the terrace.

'Why don't we have a party?' she suggested excitedly, ignoring the lack of response from the other two as she went on: 'I don't mean all the stuffed shirts of Gold Valley as we've been entertaining, but a select group of the more important people. We could bring the record player into this room and dance on the patio—have a buffet supper and so on. What do you think?'

Jinny, half resenting Lesli's use of the royal 'we', said nothing, but Bret's eyes lit up with unaccustomed enthusiasm.

'It might be an idea at that—I could fly in some people

from Vancouver and they could stay overnight.'

'Tom and Karen?' Jinny asked, her eyes brightening as she put the question to Bret across the table.

'If you'd like them to come,' he said carefully, seeming pleased when she nodded happily.

'You'll need some help with the catering,' he said in a warmer tone than he had used to her for weeks. He had evidently discounted help from Lesli, who had made little contribution to the running of the household so far.

'I'll manage,' said Jinny, suddenly shy under Bret's approving gaze. 'I enjoy cooking and baking.'

'I know you do,' he returned, surprising her. 'But you'll still need help on the night. The hostess shouldn't be tied to the kitchen.'

Embarrassed by his assumption that she would play hostess to his host, Jinny blurted out: 'Lesli socialises a lot better than I do. I'll be much happer in the kitchen.'

The warmth faded from Bret's eyes and his lips thinned out to a hard line. 'As you wish,' he said curtly, leaving the table as soon as Jinny served coffee, saying he had work to do in the office.

Jinny only half listened to Lesli's elaborate suggestions for making the party a success, her thoughts occupied with the man who sat at the big desk in the office, his dark head bent over the paperwork that occupied so many of his evening hours. Her one offer to help, shortly after their return to the ranch, had been politely rejected, and Jinny had had the feeling that he preferred the solitary peacefulness of his room to the emotion-charged atmosphere of the living room.

The desire for revenge that had prompted Jinny to force Bret into his untenable position had long since died, leaving her in a state of frozen immobility. How could she blame him for bearing the same kind of love for Lesli as she herself had nurtured for him all these years? Love, it seemed, was no respecter of persons or circumstances, lighting as it did on the most unlikely combinations, and brooking no substitutions for the ones so smitten. Mike had loved her in that way, she had loved Bret who, in his turn, loved Lesli.

But what could Jinny do, where could she go if she left Bret? She was unequipped to earn her living in a city, even if she could bring herself to leave the Valley she loved. The house at Hillside was the same as she had left it, only the animals having been brought to Valley Ranch, but the thought of living a scant three miles from the happily united Bret and Lesli filled her with despair.

Yet they could not continue to exist in this state of suspended animation. Already Jinny's clothes hung loosely on her thinned body and dark shadows lay like bruises under her eyes from the sleepless nights when she lay in the master bedroom and listened to Bret's restless tossing in the narrowness of his bed until at last she would hear the strike of a match in the stillness and know that he was awake too.

At those times the fantasies she indulged during the day were useless to her. It was almost too easy when the sun sparkled in at the windows, filling the house with its happy golden glow, to pretend that the tasks she performed with loving hands would be greeted by an equally loving husband who would sweep her into his arms when he came home for supper ... Often—too often—the desire to be held in those arms would drive her to the kitchen in the middle of the night to make a warm drink in hopes of soothing herself to sleep.

'Jinny, you haven't been listening to a word I've said,' Lesli's irritated voice broke through her reverie. 'Here I am giving you the benefit of my experience of chic parties I've given and attended—I've even had minor royalty at one or two of mine!—and I might just as well have been talking to that wall over there.'

Jinny rose and began to collect the dishes. 'This isn't exactly that kind of party, Lesli,' she remarked drily, 'I doubt if we'll even be able to scrape up one duke away out here!'

'Really, Jinny, you have no idea about the finer things of life!' her sister said fretfully, shaking her well-groomed head despairingly. 'The wife of a man like Bret should be able to support him socially, not bury herself in the kitchen like some rustic *hausfrau*. Take tonight, for instance,' she went on, her amber eyes flashing as she warmed to her subject. 'When Bret offered to get help for you, you turned him down without even understanding his motives. However ill-matched you might be, darling, Bret obviously has no wish to have his guests think he can't afford adequate help for his wife.'

Jinny sank back on to her chair, the pleasure she had felt in what she had supposed was Bret's wish to have her at his side dissipating suddenly. 'I—hadn't thought of that,' she admitted slowly.

'Of course you didn't,' soothed Lesli, a note that was almost genuine compassion in her silky voice. 'Poor lamb, you're out of your depth in this marriage, aren't you? And all because of a girlish dream you hung on to long after it had served its purpose.' She took a cigarette from the gold case beside her plate and lit it before going on: 'You must have noticed that Bret pays far more attention to me than he does to you, how different his voice is when he speaks to me. There are some things one just can't fight, Jinny, and one of them is that Bret and I belong together. We always have, but I was too young and stupid to see it at the time. I know how hurtful it must be to you, but ... be honest, sweetie,' she laid a soft hand on Jinny's and pressed it, '—you haven't even shared the same bed since he met me again, have you?'

Jinny's face flamed and she stood up abruptly. 'That was my choice,' she said stiffly, unwittingly giving Lesli the answer to her question, hurt searing through her at Bret's imparting of the knowledge to Lesli. But what else could she expect from the man who had made it abundantly clear that he remained married to her only because of her stubborn refusal to give him up? 'I'm—tired, Lesli. I think I'll go on to bed when I've seen to the dishes.'

'Good idea, darling, you don't look too bright,' Lesli commiserated without offering to help, pausing while pouring the last of the coffee into her cup to say: 'Jinny, it would be much simpler all round if you just faded out of the picture—you know what I mean? Surely it would be better for two people to be happy rather than have three utterly miserable ones? Besides,' she went on with a sidelong glance as Jinny went round the table to collect Bret's dishes, '—I doubt if you'd be on your own for long. I met a young man in town the other day who seems quite smitten with you, even though you're married.' When Jinny made no answer, she persisted: 'Mike Preston asked to be remembered.'

'Mike?'

'Yes, darling. And I must say I think you're a fool not to have snapped him up first. He's much more your type than Bret could ever be—but I gather it's not too late to pick up the pieces there if you wanted to.'

'I don't.'

Lesli shrugged. 'It was just a thought. Well, have a good night's sleep. We'll get down to planning the party properly tomorrow.'

She drifted off to the living room with her coffee and cigarette, and Jinny carried the dishes into the kitchen, her thoughts bringing a frown between her eyes as she stacked the plates and cutlery in the dishwasher. The last person she wanted to see was Mike, whose stalwart figure she had avoided on her rare visits to town by darting into the nearest store whenever she glimpsed it in the distance. It wasn't that she cared about seeing him, only that Mike above all people would know immediately that his predictions about Bret had been startlingly accurate. 'He'll break

your heart, Jinny,' he had said. 'He's not the type to stick
with one woman.'

But Mike had been wrong there in one small detail, she
reflected as she walked along the passage to her bedroom.
Bret *had* stuck to one woman emotionally all these years—
Lesli!

She showered quickly in the bathroom adjoining the
master bedroom, a bathroom she shared with Bret but at
strictly different times. Slipping on a brief flimsy nightdress, she opened the windows wide in deference to the hot
air which still lingered from the day's high temperatures
and slid between the cool sheets on the high-set bed. The
scraping of Bret's chair on the tiled floor next door gave her
a strange kind of comfort, knowing he was near, and she
was drifting off to sleep when she heard him rise and cross
the floor with an almost stealthy tread, closing it behind
him with a definite click.

Going to Lesli, she thought as sleep overtook her, tears
forcing themselves between her lids and remaining like
moondrops on her cheeks as she slept.

The following morning Jinny crossed the stable yard to the
double stall occupied by Careen and Fitz, who nuzzled her
with gentle lips as she sidled up between them. Their
change to new quarters had been made easier by the use of
this, the only double in a long row of individual stalls where
the prize Valley Ranch horses were stabled.

Jinny had turned with grateful eyes to Frank the first
time she visited the stables, but he had shaken his head and
said: 'Don't thank me, Jinny. Bret's the one who insisted
they be kept together like always.'

Nowadays the only time she saw the old horses was when
she came, as now, to saddle up Careen and trail Fitz behind, knowing he would stay close to the mare and her
steady gait as they headed for Hillside. Jinny always loosed
him a mile or so from the ranch when, with nostrils twitch-

ing, he would smell the old homestead and take off at a
frenzied gallop, Careen close at his heels.

Whinnying their pleasure at being turned into the familiar pasture, the horses grazed happily while Jinny went to
air the house, her eyes lifting automatically to the wide
stretch of blue sky above as she crossed the grassy patch in
front of the house. By some uncanny instinct, Endor seemed
to sense her presence at the ranch, and within minutes of
her arrival would be circling far above, a black speck that
suddenly fell like a stone from the sky to land with remarkable accuracy on the pasture fence. Blinking rapidly, he
would hold firmly there with his talons until she emerged
from the house.

The eagle was dismissed from her mind today as she
busied herself opening doors and windows wide. The
almost too intense heat of the past few days had been
trapped in the small living room and Jinny, feeling the
lassitude that had plagued her during the heatwave creeping insiduously into her bones, crossed to her grandfather's
chair and sat there, leaning her head back and closing her
eyes. Only here had she found some measure of peace in the
past weeks, something of her grandfather's doughty spirit
seeming to rise from the worn fibres to give her comfort.

Her eyes remained closed even when the dull roar of
Bret's returning plane vibrated against the walls of the
small house. He had gone out early on a trip mainly intended to introduce Frank to the twentieth-century manner
of ranching, he had said with a rare glint of humour in his
eyes.

He had seemed in a lighter frame of mind altogether this
morning, she reflected, even staying in the kitchen until she
came into it instead of rushing away before she made her
appearance as he usually did. Perhaps the reason for his
good humour was the long session he had spent with Lesli
last night. Jinny had awakened briefly just after one to hear
his movements from the next room, startled to hear the low

tuneless whistle that signified his contentment, but falling asleep again before her mind did more than register it. Now she felt strangely detached from the significance of that whistle; nothing really mattered any more ...

'Jinny? Jinny!'

She struggled up through the drugged mists of sleep, hearing the voice that had been prominent in the odd dream she had been having call her name. Forcing her reluctant eyelids open, she focused on the tall figure standing in the living-room doorway.

'Bret?' Her voice sounded small and childlike in the quiet room, and he came across to stand a few paces from the chair, an odd look in the light grey of his eyes:

'What are you doing here, Jinny?' he asked gently.

She blinked and looked round at the opened windows, then back up to his face. 'I—I must have fallen asleep. I came to air the house, and it was so warm in here ...'

Her voice trailed off when her eyes met and held to his as if hypnotised, and in the same way he took two more paces towards the chair and leaned over, his hands spread on the arms beside her, until his face was inches from hers.

'Jinny ...' he said huskily. 'How much longer is this to go on? I—can't take much more of it, and *you* ... look at yourself! So exhausted you fall asleep at nine in the morning, and thin as a rail because you don't eat enough to keep that eagle of yours alive. Surely you know by now that I——' He stopped and brushed a hand through his hair, ruffling its dark smoothness, then covered her hands with his and pulled her to her feet against him. She could feel the erratic beat of his heart under her palm where he held it to the light blue denim of his shirt and felt powerless to move unless it was to lay her head where her hand was.

His free hand tilted her chin up so that she was forced to meet his eyes, where an unaccustomed glow lit the grey and changed it to a translucent green. 'Listen, Jinny, Lesli and I came to an agreement last night and, provided you agree——'

A raucous croak cut harshly through the open window and Jinny pulled away to turn her head towards the source of the sound.

'That's Endor,' she said dully, then with a sharper edge to her voice: 'Something's wrong ... he sounds—strange.'

'For God's sake, Jinny, our future's at stake here, and all you can think about is a damned eagle!'

Jinny turned back to look with cold eyes at her husband. 'Endor's important to me,' she said, stressing the bird's name so pointedly that his face took on the appearance of granite.

'Meaning I'm not?'

'Meaning that I don't give a darn what agreements you and Lesli have come to,' she corrected furiously. 'The terms of this marriage stand until I decide to end them—but don't worry,' she added, coolly mocking, 'that might be sooner than you think!'

He caught her arm as she turned away and asked with ominous quietness: 'So Lesli was right when she said you'd been seeing Mike Preston again?'

'Is that what she told you?' Jinny gave a brittle laugh. 'Do you find it so unbelievable that Mike still loves me, wants to——?' She broke off and frowned. 'I have to go and see what's wrong with Endor.'

He made no effort to detain her as she walked quickly to the door, blinking back tears when the blinding sun struck her face. But the tears were forgotten when her eyes searched the paddock fence for Endor's haughty figure and found the rail empty. A movement from the ground brought her horror-stricken eyes to the dusty earth in front of the fence, and she gave a strangled cry when she saw Endor, his rounded head starkly white against the dark lower feathers, struggling towards her through the sandy soil, dragging one outstretched wing while his croaks grew fainter.

'Endor! Oh, Endor,' she sobbed, her feet moving fast towards the stricken bird, when Bret's voice came like a whiplash from behind.

'Leave him alone, Jinny! He's wild...'

Almost before the words had left his mouth the eagle gave a final squawk and collapsed on his side in the dust. Although Jinny's pace had not slackened, Bret was there before her, kneeling in his denim jeans beside the still figure of the bird.

'Is he—is he——?' she gasped, trying to avert her eyes from the inert body with its dark splotches of moisture marring the natural symmetry of feathers, but unable to do so. Bret's hands went over the bird with careful tenderness.

'No, he's not dead, but'—he rose to his feet, his knees powdered with the yellow dust—'he's badly hurt, Jinny. It's best if I put him out of his misery.'

'No! Please, Bret, help him!' Her hand came out involuntarily to clutch the smooth muscle of his forearm, warmly bronzed from the sun. For a fraction his eyes rested on her hand there, then travelled swiftly up to her ashen face.

'He's riddled with buckshot, Jinny. I doubt if he'd ever be able to fly again anyway.'

'But we must try,' she cried, the tears she had held back now flowing freely down her cheeks. 'Please?' She looked up beseechingly into his sternly set face and his eyes softened suddenly.

'All right. But I'll need some anaesthetic and something sharp to dig out the shot.'

'Couldn't we take him home? You have everything you need there.'

He looked down into her tear-streaked face, his eyes narrowed against the brilliant sun so that his expression was obscured.

'Yes, we'll take him home,' he said at last, turning away to pick up the injured bird and walk with him to the car he had parked close to the house. 'Do you have a box I can put him in?' he asked over his shoulder. 'I don't particularly relish being alone in a car with a wild creature who might come back to life at any minute.'

'I'll come with you and hold him,' Jinny offered eagerly, but he shook his head decisively.

'No. You find me a box, then close the house up and bring the horses back.'

She sped to follow his instructions, finding a disused chicken box with wire mesh stretched across its front and hurrying back to the car with it. While she helped Bret lay the inert Endor inside the box she said mournfully: 'Who would want to shoot an eagle? He's no good for eating, and doesn't harm anyone.'

'Some people will shoot at anything that moves,' he replied grimly, his eyes rising to the surrounding mountains when he had laid Endor inside the box on the back seat. 'I thought I heard shots up there early this morning.'

He repeated his instructions about closing the house and bringing in the horses, then gave her a piercing look before folding his lean form behind the wheel and driving off more carefully than usual.

By the time Jinny had secured the house and rounded up the reluctant horses to drive them back to Valley Ranch, Bret had already tended to Endor's wounds. He led her to the ten-foot-square wire enclosure where the inanimate bird lay on a bed of straw, the bright yellow hook of his beak seeming strangely pathetic in his unconscious state.

'Will he—will he live?' Jinny breathed, not looking round at the tall figure behind her.

'I don't know, Jinny,' he said quietly. 'Wild creatures of his age don't usually survive in confinement.'

'He will! ... he must!' she vowed passionately as she hooked her fingers into the mesh and stared at Endor as if willing him to live. Unarticulated in her mind was the link between the sweet simplicity of her own past, in which the eagle had played a part, and the heartaching reality of the present. If Endor died, something in her would die too.

CHAPTER EIGHT

JINNY put the finishing touches to the long dining-room table and stood back to look appraisingly at the écru lace tablecloth bedecked with low bowls of summer flowers. She had already checked the silverware and napkins placed conveniently near the stack of rose-patterned plates, and turning from the doorway she pictured the table as it would look when she brought out the colourful bowls of salad, the succulent pink ham of massive proportions and thickly sliced beef from their own Valley Ranch cows.

Satisfied, she sped along the corridor, unfastening her tunic top as she went. Already the sound of masculine voices raised in talk and bursts of laughter came from the living room where Bret was entertaining Tom and the two men who had flown in from Vancouver with him and Karen.

A smile curved Jinny's lips as she picked up the towels Bret had soaked after his shower, stuffing them into the hamper before taking a clean one for herself. The pleasure she had felt in seeing Karen's blonde head descend from the aircraft had been topped by the news Karen had imparted in her room later.

'I have to tell somebody, Jinny, or I'll burst,' she said, turning sparkling eyes to the darker girl. 'Tom and I are— well, *I'm* going to have a baby!'

'Oh, Karen, that's wonderful!' Jinny exclaimed softly, feeling only a faint wistfulness as she hugged Karen. 'You must be so happy—is Tom pleased?'

'Like a man who's just inherited a million dollars,' Karen laughed. 'Just wait till you have the same kind of news for Bret, Jinny. You'll know what I mean.'

'Yes ... yes, I suppose so.'

Karen picked up the forlorn note in her voice and looked sharply at her. 'Jinny, are you feeling okay? I mean, you look a little peaky—and surely you've lost weight since I last saw you?'

Jinny forced a smile. 'I'm fine. There's an awful lot to do on a ranch, that's all.'

'And I don't suppose that sister of yours does much to help!' the fair girl returned shrewdly. 'How long does she propose staying with you and Bret?'

'Oh—a few weeks. I think,' Jinny replied evasively, and moved to the door. 'If you need anything, just yell.'

'Yes—thanks, I will.'

Afraid that her face would reveal the truth Karen's thoughtful look seemed to suspect, Jinny had made her escape.

Now, after a hurried shower, she dressed in the bedroom, slipping over her head last of all a calf-length dress of gossamer-fine polyester chiffon in a dark royal blue which made instant drama of her eyes. The dress was styled to fit closely as far as the hips before frothing out extravagantly above ankles made more slender by the high-heeled sandals she had bought to match the dress. It was one she had bought on her shopping spree in Vancouver before the wedding, and she wondered now as she looked into the full-length mirror if it wasn't too revealing for a simple house party for friends and neighbours. The white rise of her breasts was clearly visible, shoelace straps formed into a halter round her neck having been designed more for decoration than support.

She shrugged her shoulders and clasped a wide silver band round her wrist. What did it matter anyway? Bret would have eyes for no one but Lesli, and there was no other man whose opinion she cared about.

Since the morning at Hillside ten days ago when he had gone to Endor's aid, Bret had become even more morosely uncommunicative, even Lesli's bright chatter at the dinner table eliciting little response. Whether or not he expanded on those nights, which were becoming more frequent, when Jinny left them with last drinks on the patio while she went to bed, she was gradually schooling herself not to think about. All she knew was that Bret no longer made any pretence of accompanying her to the big master bedroom at bedtime.

Jinny was thankful for Karen's company as she went into the living room and found all eyes focused on them. Karen's long A-line dress in rose pink was a perfect foil for the vibrant dark blue of Jinny's, and the men took in the picture silently until Tom moved towards them.

'Well, if that isn't a bevy of beauty, I don't know what is,' he said heartily, slipping an arm round Karen's waist and smiling at Jinny. Bret stayed with the two younger men who had flown in with Tom and Karen, a glass held loosely in one hand and a lit cigar in the other. Jinny's eyes touched briefly on his dark good looks in a suit that was the colour of his hair and a shirt so white that his skin by contrast seemed a dusky brown.

In return, his eyes ran quickly over her white shoulders and down to her feet, a frown creasing his brows when they paused at the low-cut neckline, but when they rose again to meet Jinny's he looked down into the liquid in his glass.

'No wonder you wanted to keep your bride away out here, hidden from my lecherous eyes,' said Tom Drake, the younger of the two men Bret had introduced as business acquaintances, his blue eyes twinkling as Jinny followed Tom and Karen across the room. 'If you ever get tired of this air jockey, Jinny, I'll be available.'

'Thanks, I'll keep it in mind,' she said lightly. 'But don't commit yourself until you've met my sister, she's——'

'Can I get you something to drink?' Bret put in bluntly, his bleak look encompassing both Jinny and Karen.

'Just a soft drink for Karen, if you will, Bret,' Tom said quickly, his mouth widening into a proud smile when he looked at his wife. 'She's on the wagon for the next few months.'

'Oh?' Bret's eyebrows lifted as he looked from one to the other.

'*Tom!*' Karen reproved, but her eyes were softly luminous as she looked up into her husband's glowing face.

'Everybody's going to know before too long, anyway, honey,' he cajoled, looking over to Bret. 'If you'll get those drinks, Bret, I'd like to make a toast.'

A smile hovered behind Bret's grey eyes as he turned away to the array of bottles and glasses on a portable buffet behind him and busied himself pouring the drinks for the two women and replenishing the men's glasses. He had not asked Jinny her preference, but made her normal weak-toned drink. The smile faded from his eyes when her fingers brushed his as she took the glass from him.

'So what's the toast, Tom?' he asked abruptly.

Tom held his glass up, intoning seriously: 'To motherhood and—heaven help the poor child!—my son or daughter who's due to make an appearance some time in February.'

A chorus of male congratulation broke about Tom's head, and Jinny felt tears prick her eyes as she looked at the proud Tom and ecstatic Karen, who gazed up at him adoringly. Her eyes met Bret's as she raised her glass to her lips and the cool rim checked its upward rise as they stared at each other as if they were alone in the room. Then with a quick movement Bret lifted his stubby glass and drained the whisky it held in one gulp.

'I couldn't let you beat me to it, Bret,' Tom chuckled.

'After all, Karen and I have been married for four years now.'

'You didn't have to rush on my account,' Bret said tersely. 'Children—my own—don't figure in my scheme of things.'

'Oh, come on, Bret,' said Hank Linden, his brown eyes serious behind thick-rimmed glasses. Of the two men Bret claimed as business friends, Jinny preferred this quietly intense one, who seemed to look from an inner solitude to observe the doings of his fellows. 'All men want to perpetuate themselves, it's a natural instinct.'

'Then I'm afraid I'll have to admit to being unnatural,' Bret retorted, his head turning to look over Jinny's to the doorway when Lesli's voice floated across the room.

'Well said, Bret! There are far too many people running around perpetuating themselves all over the place.'

As she posed against the entrance, Lesli's dress of flame-coloured wispy chiffon created an effect that must have been far beyond her wildest dreams. A silence fell over the group of people who stood watching as she drifted further into the room, veils of chiffon trailing languidly behind her. When she reached Bret she laid a hand on his arm and said throatily: 'I'd love a drink, darling, if you're playing bartender.'

Bret let her hand fall away from his arm as he moved to the trolley to fix the drink, obviously having no need to ask her preference either. Karen's eyes went in a puzzled way from his back to Jinny's bent head, then back to where Lesli waited with a confident smile for Bret's return.

Breaking the sudden silence that had fallen on the group, Karen said coolly: 'I think you missed the news that Tom and I are expecting a baby, Lesli. That's why we were——'

'Oh, how dreary for you!' Lesli exclaimed, smiling up at Bret as he put a chartreuse-coloured glass into her hand. 'But there are ways, you know.'

'Ways?' Karen echoed blankly. 'Ways for doing what?'

'Let me introduce Hank Linden and Tim Drake,' Bret interposed smoothly, taking Lesli's elbow in a firm grip as he turned to the two men who had been staring openly at her since her entrance. 'You were out when they arrived.'

Lesli went into a laughingly derogative description of the Gold Valley hairdresser, omitting her furious outburst to Jinny and Karen on her return that the stupid girl had made such a mess of it she would have to do it again herself. The men had been out with Bret, who had shown them round the ranch buildings while Jinny and Karen prepared a light dinner, so they had not witnessed her white-faced temper.

The sound of wheels crunching on the gravelled forecourt brought Bret round just as Jinny bent to put her drink on the coffee table beside her. His elbow cracked against her temple, knocking her off balance so that she staggered as she straightened. Bret's hands shot out to grasp her shoulders, his eyes showing quick concern as he held her slightly away from him.

'I'm sorry. Are you all right?'

'Yes, I'm—fine,' she answered breathlessly, though distant bells seemed to be ringing in her head. How much of that was due to the blow or to the fact that Bret's hands on her bare shoulders were sending a shivering warmth through her she wouldn't have been prepared to say.

'Come on, Bret,' Tom joked from behind them as the front doorbell rang, 'you've no time to kiss it better now— your guests are here.'

Bret's eyes dropped from Jinny's face and he looked surprised to find his hands still grasping her soft flesh, but his fingers tightened momentarily before he released her and walked with her to the door, one arm loosely round her waist.

'I can manage,' she said in a low voice, and felt his arm grow firmer as he looked down at her.

'Can you?' he asked enigmatically. 'I wish——'

He broke off when they reached the door and the bell rang again with an impatient chime. Keeping one arm round her waist, he leaned forward to open the door, and Jinny was left to wonder what it was that he wished.

Most of the older couples drifted back to the living room after supper, the younger ones preparing to dance again on the flower-bordered terrace where Bret had lit open-flame patio lights at intervals round the edges. Satisfied from the numerous compliments flying her way that the buffet she had prepared had been a success, Jinny began to stack the dishes while Bret put a record on the stereo set placed near the open glass doors to the terrace.

'Leave that,' said Karen in a peremptory voice that brooked no argument. 'Go and dance with your husband— you haven't danced together all evening. There's a limit to being a good host and hostess, and this is it!'

Bret turned from the stereo and held out a hand to Jinny. 'I was about to say the same thing,' he said evenly. 'That's why I put this record on.'

Jinny hesitated for only a moment before putting her hand in his and following him out to the patio, her heart's beat thrown out of rhythm when he took her in his arms and pulled her close. The music from the dining room was slowly sensuous, and beyond the flickering light of the lamps a velvet sky, studded with a million brilliant stars, seemed to stretch in a never-ending dome over them. An involuntary sigh escaped Jinny's lips and she felt her hand being lifted to rest on Bret's chest where his shirt met his jacket, his own hand holding it there as if he feared she would draw it away.

At the same time, his other hand moved up from her waist and over the cool softness of her skin to the nape of her neck, where he applied a light pressure to bring her head closer to his waiting cheek. As his jaw nuzzled gently against the smooth silk of her hair, Jinny felt a wildly hysterical desire to laugh. Whatever his reasons for wooing her in this particular way—whether to put on a show of marital unity for the benefit of the guests, or to soften her up for the great letdown—she was powerless to question it at that moment. Her bones were melting to water against his relaxed yet vibrantly alive body, every sense tingling with awareness of him...

'So this is where you are!' Lesli's voice, sharpened with annoyance, came as a douse of cold water and caused Jinny's head to jerk sharply away from Bret's, the dreaminess in her eyes being replaced with shocked wonder as she saw the broad figure behind her sister in the doorway.

'Mike!' she gasped, and felt Bret's arms drop from her.

'You should take better care of your guests, Jinny,' said Lesli waspishly. 'Even if he is a late arrival.'

'Sorry I couldn't get here sooner, Jinny,' said Mike, stepping forward so that he stood between her and Bret. 'I was on duty till nine.'

Jinny stared helplessly at him. She hadn't asked Mike to the party, but he evidently thought she had. Lesli had done most of the inviting—*Lesli!* Jinny looked sharply at her sister, who gazed innocently back at her as she moved to take Bret's arm.

'You can finish the dance with me, Bret, while Jinny takes care of her guest.'

'But I——' Jinny protested, but her voice died away as Bret, giving a tight-lipped nod to Mike, took Lesli into his arms and moved off with her.

'Did I come at an awkward time?' Mike asked quietly, drawing her attention back from the hurtful picture of Lesli's chiffon-draped figure being held with almost fierce closeness to Bret's.

'I—no. No, Mike. Would you like something to eat? I think there's a little left.'

'If it's not too much trouble. I wasn't able to get away from the office for a dinner hour.'

With a last glance to where Bret and Lesli had disappeared into the group of dancers, Jinny led the way into the dining room and herself piled a plate high with leftovers from the table.

'Come into the kitchen, Mike,' she said dully, picking up a stack of used dishes. 'You can talk to me while I see to these.'

He followed her and sat at the dinette table with his plate while she rinsed the plates under the tap and stacked them in the machine. There was something soothing to her in his casual talk of Valley people as he attacked his plate with a healthy appetite, and gradually her nerves calmed to the point where she made a laughingly caustic remark about the town spinster who had recently become engaged to a lumberjack working in the area.

The machine hummed busily over the first batch of dishes and Jinny came to lean against the counter beside the table, her smile fading when Mike rose and came to stand in front of her, his light blue eyes probing as they looked into hers.

'Are you happy, Jinny?' he asked quietly.

'What a question to ask a bride of seven weeks!' she laughed shakily, straightening to turn away from the searching gaze that threatened to reach into the trembling recesses of her heart, but his hands lifted to her shoulders and forced her round to face him.

'Nevertheless, I'm asking it,' he said tightly. 'From what your sister says——'

'Oh, don't pay any attention to Lesli,' she laughed with forced lightness. 'As my older sister, she's prejudiced.'

'Well, I can't say that I'm not prejudiced too, but it seems to me you're far too thin and worried looking to be a happily married bride. Tell me honestly, Jinny,' he raised her chin with firm fingers, 'is it true that your sister and Bret are—that you don't live with him as his wife?'

Jinny gasped, humiliation rushing over her in waves.

How could Lesli have talked about such intimate matters to a man who was a virtual stranger to her? It wasn't as if she needed the extra boost to her confidence that Bret loved her—she must know that he was hers for the asking. Perhaps it was that Lesli, never one to wait for something she wanted, was growing impatient and more anxious to get rid of Jinny. What better way than to throw in her way a man who had obviously confessed to loving her?

'Bret would never . . . do that,' she quavered, ignoring the second part of Mike's question. 'No matter how much he cared for——' Her voice choked, and he muttered an oath.

As the dishwasher paused in its cycle, creating an oasis of silence round them, he said exasperatedly:

'I'm not going to say "I told you so", though I could, it seems. I knew he wasn't the kind for a girl like you. Listen, Jinny,' he went on urgently, 'I've applied for a posting to Alberta, and I heard this week that I'm to be transferred in September. Come with me, Jinny. Forget——'

'I can't, Mike,' she wailed, tears spilling over to roll down her cheeks, Mike's jacket rough under her cheek as he pulled her fiercely to him. 'I—I still love . . .'

Her last word was lost in the sudden reactivation of the dishwasher, but Bret's voice came across with harsh clarity from the door.

'Some of our guests are leaving, if you can spare the time to see them off!'

Jinny stiffened and pulled herself from Mike's sheltering arms, which seemed reluctant to let her go. By the time she had brushed away the tears blurring her vision, Bret had gone.

'Come with me now, Jinny,' Mike urged, countering her vaguely shocked look with: 'I'll find somewhere for you to live in town until I leave, and then as soon as you're free we'll be married. Jinny?'

The rise in his voice was addressed to her back as she went towards the door. Pausing there to blow her nose and dab at her eyes, she turned to say huskily:

'I'm sorry, Mike. If you only knew how much I wish I could love you—but I can't. If you love me only half as much as I ... love Bret ... then you'll understand.'

The two older couples who were leaving together were already saying their farewells to Bret on the front doorstep, and as Jinny came up the silver-haired rancher husband of an elegantly groomed woman said: 'And here's the lucky lady who'll be taking that trip to Europe with you! Don't forget to ask me over to see your new stock, Bret!'

'Maybe the Staffords would be coming over to see *our* new stock, Harvey, if you were just half as adventurous as Bret here!' his wife put in tartly before turning to Jinny. 'Goodnight, my dear, and thank you for a lovely party. You and Bret must be sure to come and see us soon.'

Jinny forced a smile, feeling Bret's cool eyes on her face. 'Yes, we will. Thank you for coming.'

When the door closed at last she looked up into Bret's closed expression. 'What did he mean—a trip to Europe?'

Bret shrugged and walked past her. 'Just that I've planned a cattle buying trip to France and Scotland in the autumn, when I hope to be able to buy some in stock to start a herd.' He stopped, his eyes looking sardonically into hers when she caught up with him. 'They automatically assumed it was you I intend to take with me. Foolish of them, wasn't it?'

His shoulders were tautly erect as he entered the dining room, narrowly missing Mike as he came along the passage from the kitchen.

'I'm leaving now, Jinny.' Mike checked his stride and looked sombrely at her. 'If you need me—well, you know where to find me.'

She stared numbly after his retreating back, feeling strangely bereft in knowing that he would not come again unless she asked him to. The party had scarcely been a happy occasion for him, and even less so for herself, tied as

she was by the unreasoning bonds of love to one man while
the other, who would have been only too willing to love and
cherish her, walked away from her.

'Come on, Jinny,' said Karen from the doorway, her
cheeks flushed to a delicate pink matching her dress. 'Bret's
just announced the last dance, so come and grab him before
some other designing female does.'

At the other end of the room Jinny saw Bret's head bent
to Lesli's laughingly upraised face, although there was no
answering smile on his.

'No—no, I'll make some coffee,' she said quickly, turning away.

Karen pulled her back by the arm and marched her over
to where Lesli was taking Bret's hand to lead him out to the
terrace. 'Don't make such a drudge of yourself,' Karen said
forcefully. 'There's plenty of time for coffee afterwards.
Here's your partner, Bret—and why don't you make one of
those nice single young men happy by dancing with him,
Lesli?'

The furious Lesli was borne away by the exuberant
Karen, and Jinny and Bret were left studiously avoiding
each other's eyes.

'Why the hell doesn't she mind her own business?' he
said at last in a low, blistering tone.

'She ... she doesn't know that we ... that ...' Jinny
stopped, lost for words, then turned and said in a small
voice: 'I'll make some coffee before everyone leaves.'

'No!' His hand grasped her wrist in a bruising hold and
she paused, keeping her head averted from him. 'We'll pre-
serve Karen's and everyone else's illusions—for tonight,
anyway.'

She made no resistance when he led her to the patio,
where a dozen or so other couples were moving dreamily in
time to the music. Lesli, her face frozen into immobility,
was being steered round by an earnest Hank Linden, and
Karen nestled dreamily in Tom's arms.

This time, there was a definite gap between their bodies when Bret put his arms round Jinny and led her into the oblivious dancers. They danced in painful silence for some time until Jinny, unable to bear the mounting tension, burst out:

'Bret, I know you're as miserable as I am about—the way things are. Tonight when I talked with Mike I realised——'

'Yes, I heard what you realised,' he said shortly, seeming not to notice her tightened grip on his hand or her head jerking sharply up towards his. He had *heard* her admission that she still loved him? Her mind whirled away in such a dizzying spiral that she almost missed his next words.

'. . . seems to me that the best thing all round is for us to put an end to this farce of a marriage.' The deadly calm of his voice betrayed no emotion whatsoever. 'There's no point in carrying on when one of the parties is committed elsewhere.'

'No . . . no, I suppose not.' She took a deep breath and looked up into his face, the flickering patio lamps emphasising the shadows under his high-planed cheekbones and totally obscuring the expression in his deep-set eyes. If she had wanted proof that her admission of love for him left him cold, it was evident in the aloof set of his head, his impersonal hold as he led her like an automaton round the flagstoned terrace. Pain gathered like a ball of sharp-pointed thorns round her heart when she realised that the half-acknowledged dream she had cherished, that he would in some miraculous way come to accept the love she felt for him in every fibre of her being, was no more than that—the wishful thinking of an idealistic girl.

'Any time you want to——' she began, stopping when betraying tears thickened her voice.

'It's never been a question of what I want,' he said brusquely after a momentary silence. 'Freedom for both of us lies with you.'

His words hung in the air in the pregnant hush that followed the ending of the record, then suddenly a babble of voices broke out. 'One more, Bret—you can't want to finish the party this soon. It's Sunday tomorrow, we can all sleep late.'

Jinny broke away, murmuring about coffee, and as she reached the kitchen she heard another record start, its strains even more conducive to the romantic end of a lovers' evening. From the kitchen window she looked out to the patio on her right, seeing only the outer rim of dancers in the fitful light thrown from the kerosene lamps. Karen's fair head, almost indistinguishable from Tom's as it pressed against her hair, came and went into the deeper shadows, followed closely by Bret and Lesli, the world seemingly forgotten as he spoke seriously into her upraised face.

Telling her that their waiting period was almost over?

CHAPTER NINE

'You should let that bird go, Jinny,' Frank Milner's deep voice came from behind her, and Jinny spun round with a half-guilty look on her face.

'He's really not well enough yet,' she protested weakly, turning back to the wire mesh chicken run where Endor flapped his wings and regarded them with watchful yellow eyes.

'That's not true and you know it,' Frank persisted bluntly, moving forward to stand beside her, his eyes appraising the eagle's frustrated wing sweeps. 'He's been ready for a week or more.'

Stung by his automatic assumption about the bird she felt was hers, Jinny snapped: 'I'll let him go when I'm good and ready! You don't know anything about eagles, Frank.'

'Only enough to know that you can't keep a wild creature longer than he has a mind to stay,' he replied laconically, then chuckled unexpectedly. 'Reminds me of my wife——'

'Your *wife*?' she gasped, looking for the first time into the harsh lines of his weatherbeaten face. 'I—I didn't know you'd been married, Frank.'

He shrugged. 'It was a long time ago, I don't talk about it any more.' His voice softened as he nodded to the cage and went on: 'She was like that, wild and untamed, wanting to be in a place I had no part of. It wasn't any use trying to hold her,' he ended with a sigh, then cocked an eye at Jinny. 'Any more than you can hold *him*.'

Jinny looked after the ranch manager's broad-shouldered back as he sauntered away, shaken by the knowledge that he, too, had known the heartache of a love that was useless against the yearning of another human being to be elsewhere. She didn't quite know if the welling up of sympathy in her heart was for the kindly ranch manager or for herself—perhaps it was a little of both.

As she turned away from the cage she caught a glimpse of the Stafford pick-up pulling away from the front of the house, and a thoughtful frown marked her brow as she crossed the roughly cut hay meadow lying alongside the stables. Tim Drake and Hank Linden had stayed on at the ranch after Tom and Karen went back to Vancouver, and spent most of their days travelling round the countryside looking into the history of the area, they said.

If only for the reason that their presence made it easier for Jinny to postpone making a decision about leaving Valley Ranch, she was glad of their lighthearted company at the dinner table. Lesli, too, expanded under their obvious male interest in her anecdotes about her own travels and people she had met, so that the silence between Bret and Jinny went unremarked.

Sighing, she went into the house by the kitchen door. Whether it had been obvious to the others or not, Bret's

attitude of polite coolness towards herself since the party
had made it abundantly clear that he was barely tolerating
her presence in the house. Any hope she had nourished that
he would at last come to realise and accept her love had
died when he had admitted to hearing her admission of that
love to Mike and humiliatingly rejected it minutes later.
But in her heart she could hardly blame him for his attitude
—Mike loved her in the same hopeless way, irritating her
although he didn't share the same roof with her. How much
more frustrating it must be for Bret to live in the same
house with two women who loved him, while his heart was
committed to only one of them?

The already overpowering heat of the day had made
Jinny uncomfortably aware that she was overdressed in long-
sleeved blouse and slacks, and she went noiselessly along
the carpeted passage to her bedroom with the intention of
changing into shorts and halter top before spending some
time in the garden. Perhaps another shower would cool her
off and wash away the lethargic feeling already creeping
into her limbs.

A muffled exclamation from the next room halted her
steps and turned her head to the connecting door between
Bret's office and the bedroom.

Sliding off her low-heeled sandals, she padded in her
bare feet past the wide master bed to the closed door into
the office, laying an ear against the wooden panel and hearing the stealthy closing of a drawer. Bret? No. His movements were always forceful, decisive . . . never stealthy.

Jinny turned the handle quietly and opened the door, her
eyes widening when she saw Lesli's robed figure at the
desk, a sheet of writing paper in her hand. The waving line
of her long brown hair jerked sharply round when Jinny
gasped:

'Lesli! What are you doing? This is Bret's office!'

For a moment Lesli looked nonplussed, then anger
blazed in her eyes as she shook the paper towards Jinny.

'It might be his office, but this concerns *us*,' she exploded violently. Her voice dropped to a less abrasive note when Jinny opened the door further and stepped towards the desk. 'Do you remember my saying I couldn't understand why Bret married you? Well,' she shook the paper again, 'here's the reason.'

A sudden premonition brought Jinny's hand up as if to ward off a blow. 'No—I don't want to read it.'

'Then I'll read it to you,' Lesli snapped, holding the paper closer to her eyes as she recited in a crisp monotone:

'I, Denis Stephen O'Brien, being of sound mind, do hereby bequeath my property known as Hillside Ranch in the County of Gold Valley, British Columbia, and all its rights in mineral and real property, to Bret Philip Stafford, on the sole condition that he marry my granddaughter, Virginia Clare O'Brien, within six months of my death. This will takes precedence over . . .'

Lesli's voice faded into the background as blood pounded in Jinny's ears, almost blocking the faint memory of her grandfather's last words to her the night he died. 'Good. Then I've done the right thing.' He had known of her love for Bret and tried to secure her happiness by dangling the carrot of Hillside gold before Bret's eyes! But Bret . . .

'Bret—never believed in Hillside gold,' she said faintly, and Lesli stopped her restless pacing round the room.

'No?' she asked scornfully. 'Then why else did he bring two geologists out here to go over it inch by inch?'

'Geol——? What are you talking about, Lesli?'

'I've suspected all week that those two "business friends" of Bret's didn't know him as well as he led us to believe, and last night Tim let slip that he and Hank Linden work for a mining exploration company in the city. It doesn't take a genius to work out why Bret wanted them down here—this proves it.' Like a terrier with a rat between its teeth, Lesli waved the piece of paper, then held it still and looked thoughtfully at it. 'But why has Bret been sweet-talking me into selling him my half of Hillside when he had this? All he had to do was marry you and—Jinny?'

Her voice went up to a high-pitched scream when Jinny crumpled and fell face down on the floor at her feet.

Oblivion came as a relief to Jinny's consciousness, blotting out the stark hurt that Lesli's words brought, and she fought against returning to reality even when icy water trickled from a weight on her brow to mingle with her hair.

'Jinny? Snap out of it, Jinny! Help me get you up.'

Jinny's eyes fluttered open with reluctance and she looked bewilderedly into Lesli's straining face as she leaned over and tugged under her arms.

'I'm ... all right,' she murmured, struggling to rise to her feet and threatening to collapse again as soon as she did so.

'Oh, come along,' Lesli panted irritably, taking Jinny's weight and supporting her to the narrow bed.

'No! Not here,' Jinny begged feebly when Lesli half threw her on to the bed.

'If you think I'm going to carry you into your own bed you're mistaken!' Lesli pushed her head roughly down on the white pillow and lifted her feet to drop them on the dark blue coverlet, a scornful glint in her eyes as she straightened. 'If I didn't know better, I'd say——' She broke off abruptly and her eyes widened as she looked down into Jinny's pale face and closed eyes. 'That's it, isn't it? You're pregnant!'

Jinny's eyes flew open and focused on the furious set of her sister's good-looking face.

'That—can't be,' she breathed, but even as the denial left her lips she knew with frightening clarity that what Lesli had stated was true. The lethargy she had been fighting off for days past, the disruption in a previously healthy physical cycle—these she had explained away by blaming the unnaturally strained living conditions since her marriage. Now the certainty that she carried Bret's child under her heart washed over her in a warm wave of wonder, tenderness reaching with delicate fingers to encompass every part of her body.

Lesli's lips tightened to a hard line when she read the truth in Jinny's suddenly luminous eyes.

'You little fool,' she hissed. 'Didn't you know enough to——?' She broke off and swung away angrily.

'You don't understand, Lesli.' Jinny raised herself to one elbow and looked entreatingly at her sister's tightly coiled frame leaning against the desk. 'I *want* this baby, I *need*——'

'Oh, yes, I know what you need a baby for,' Lesli interrupted jerkily, giving a harsh laugh as she turned to face Jinny. 'But you're way off if you think a child will tie Bret to you! He'll run a thousand miles in the other direction! You heard him yourself last night.'

Jinny fell back on the pillow again, suddenly weak as reality rushed in to replace the euphoric bliss of a moment before. Had she in her deepest heart hoped that Bret would miraculously come to love her as the mother of his child? If she had, remembrance shattered the hope into a million pieces. How many times had he stated flatly that there would be no sons from him to carry on at Valley Ranch? His aversion to fatherhood ran much deeper, she knew, than the unwillingness to take on responsibility which Lesli implied.

Lesli had thrown herself into a chair by the desk, her brow knitted in thought, her hands clenching and unclenching on the arms of the chair. Minutes passed until at last she rose and came across to the bed, her voice coolly controlled.

'Listen, Jinny, I've worked out why Bret hasn't brought this will forward before. He wanted me here, and knew I wouldn't come if I knew that Pop had left everything to him. Don't you see?' she interrupted herself impatiently when Jinny stared up at her with confused eyes. 'He needed an excuse to get me here, and what better than pretending he wanted to buy my share of Hillside for some non-existent cattle breeding experiment he said he wanted to do at Hillside?'

'But . . . I think he does want to . . .'

'Nonsense!' Lesli bit off sharply. 'He's beginning to realise what I've known all along—that he's not cut out to be a rancher. In fact, I wonder if he ever did seriously think of taking it up again. All he's really interested in is that airline of his, and just think of the ways he could expand if gold is found at Hillside . . . maybe even a passenger line all over the world. That could make him a very important man, Jinny, and to someone like Bret, that's his life's blood.'

Jinny turned her head on the pillow that still held the faint scent of Bret, and tears thickened her voice. 'He's already an important man to—the Valley.'

Lesli waved a dismissing hand. 'What's the Valley compared to world-wide recognition as an astute man of business? You'll have to admit,' she laughed with renewed confidence as she picked up the paper bearing their grandfather's shaky handwriting, 'you won't find a more astute businessman than Bret!'

That was true, Jinny thought bitterly, her tears turning to ice in her veins. It seemed Bret was willing to go to any lengths to get what he wanted, even to spending evening after boring evening playing chess with an old man who loved him so unreservedly he had given his granddaughter and his dream of years into his hands. Bret had mocked that dream of gold, to her if not to her grandfather, when all the time he had . . .

'I think it's better you don't mention any of this—including the baby business—until I've had a chance to find out what's going on,' Lesli went on with breezy sureness, folding the paper in her hand as she perched on the edge of the bed beside Jinny. 'Bret's flying Hank and Tim back to

Vancouver in the morning, and I mean to go with them.' She held up the folded paper. 'I'll take this with me and find out just how legal it is ... in fact, I might find out that you could get a very good divorce settlement on the strength of it. It's positively archaic of Pop to have handed you over as part of a business deal.'

'I don't want any settlement from Bret,' said Jinny, her voice shakily low.

'Nevertheless, darling, you should look out for your own interests.' There was a hint of genuine compassion in Lesli's amber eyes as she looked down at her sister. 'Even though Bret and I—well, you're my little sister, and I wouldn't want you to suffer because you fell for the wrong man and made it easy for him to make a fool of you. You *did* make it rather obvious, sweetie, even when you were young. We often laughed about Jinny's schoolgirl passion for an older man—oh, not unkindly, of course. You were too sweet for that.'

Jinny's hands clenched so hard that her nails bit into her palms, but she said nothing.

'Of course, you'll want to make arrangements for'— Leslie paused delicately—'well, you won't want to keep the child, will you? It would be a constant reminder of how foolish you'd been.'

'That's where you're mistaken, Lesli,' Jinny said with alien harshness, causing Lesli's eyes to flicker with sudden uncertainty over her face. 'The child will be a constant reminder to me, yes, but Bret will also be reminded of his slick business practices every year when I send him a picture on his son's, or daughter's, birthday!'

Lesli had grown visibly paler, and she moistened her lips nervously. 'Don't be silly, Jinny. What good would that accomplish? You'd be using the child to punish Bret—I'd hardly have thought that was your style.'

'My style has changed quite a lot lately, thanks to you and Bret,' Jinny retorted bitterly, swinging her feet to the

floor as Lesli stood up, incensed. She put out a hand automatically when Jinny swayed dizzily.

'You're not yourself, darling. Here, let me help you to
bed, and I insist you stay there for the rest of the day. I'll
see to the men's meals.'

Jinny had no strength to resist the tempting coolness of
the sheets on the wide bed, and she allowed Lesli to support
her into the adjoining room but waved away further offers
of help. Lesli's overly-sweet solicitude had come far too
late, she reflected sourly, to do anything more than raise
suspicions as to her motives.

'Well, I'll ... um ... bring you some lunch on a tray
when you're settled in.'

Jinny gave her a venomous look. 'I don't want anything
to eat. Just leave me alone.'

Lesli shrugged and swept through the doorway in her
full-skirted robe, closing the door with a decisive snap behind her.

When she had dragged herself to the bathroom, Jinny
stood under the cooling spray of the shower for long
minutes, letting the water run over her face and through her
hair until gradually the pounding pain in her head lessened
and she could think more clearly. Taking a fresh towel from
the rack after drying herself, she went on bare feet back to
the bedroom and selected the briefest nightdress she possessed to slip over her head. There was more than a hint of
thunder in the air, although outside the open window the
sun still shone with unending brilliance. But long experience of how quickly the mountain scene could change made
her sure that the rains would come soon, bringing blessed
relief from the oppressive heat.

She slid between the sheets after throwing the blankets
back, sighing her weariness as her head sank into the softness of her pillow. Familiar sounds of ranch life came
faintly through the window and soothed rather than dis-
turbed her. There was the high-spirited whinnying of

Prince, the black colt which was the pride of Valley Ranch,
when he was released into the tree-shaped paddock beside
the stables; the indignant protests of a mother cow newly
parted from her calf; and a man's chivvying cries designed
to move the mother on.

The man wasn't Bret. He had ridden out with Frank to
an unknown destination early that morning, and wouldn't
return until late afternoon. Bret! For the first time since
Lesli had read their grandfather's will, Jinny let her mind
conjure up the lean, well-knit figure of the man who had
married her without being in love with her, who had
brought ecstasy to her for one short night, and whose child
lay now in the protection of her body.

She waited for the searing wave of hatred to engulf her,
but there was only the pain of deep regret to bruise her
heart when his face rose behind her closed lids, dissolving
and reappearing as her memory led her back through the
years to the time when she had first known that she loved
him. Her dewy-eyed budding womanhood had been
attracted to his laughing eyes, his sheer exuberance in being
alive in a world he loved.

Another picture rose before her eyes, of the way Bret
looked now, his face hollowed out to shadowed clefts under
too prominent cheekbones, deep lines scoring each side of
his tightly held mouth which, even when it smiled, never
brought warmth to the bleak grey of his eyes.

Tears oozed slowly from under her lids and ran down her
cheeks, tasting salty on her lips. Marriage to her had done
this to Bret, her childish longing for revenge twisting all
their lives so that none of them was happy. Whatever his
motive for marrying her had been, she knew he was as helpless against his love for Lesli as she herself was against hers
for him.

Lesli's face, contorted into a witchlike mask, loomed horribly near and Jinny clutched the child to her breast, ward-

ing off the elongated hands that reached to tear him from her while Lesli mocked in a sing-song chant: 'Give him up, Jinny, Bret doesn't want him. I'll get rid of him for you, give him to me...'

'No!' Jinny screamed as the child, his dark hair a cloud round his head and grey eyes laughing, slipped from her grasp. 'Bret! Bret! Don't let her take him! Bret!'

'Jinny! Wake up, Jinny, you're dreaming ... it's just a dream, honey.'

Her horror-filled eyes looked up into Bret's anxious face and she threw herself against him, her arms going under his open shirt to clutch fiercely round his back as she sobbed: 'Don't let her take him, Bret ... he's so lovely ...'

'Take who, Jinny?' he asked gently, sitting on the edge of the bed and cradling her shaking body against his, his arms firm around her.

'The b——'

Her breath was released suddenly in a strangled sob when reality forced its way into her sleep-drugged mind. The warm flesh under her cheek, the soothing motion of a jaw against her hair, were no figments of a dream world. She jerked herself abruptly out of Bret's arms and fell back against the pillow.

'I—I must have been dreaming,' she said dazedly, lifting one hand to rub her furrowed brow. 'I'm—sorry.'

'You don't have to be,' he told her briefly, staying where he was, his thigh warm and hard and strangely comforting through the sheet. 'We all have bad dreams at times.'

She managed a wan smile. 'This was a dilly! So real, I still feel...'

Her eyes wandered from his face to the open shirt where his chest hair curled damply over his lightly bronzed skin. The same warm moisture was still detectably on her hands from his back and she said contritely: 'You must be dying for a cold shower.'

'I was just about to take one when I heard you call me.

I—didn't realise at first that you were dreaming.' The husky softness in his voice was echoed in the opaque gleam of his eyes as they searched her face. 'Lesli tells me you're not feeling well—what is it, the heat?'

'Yes, the heat,' she agreed with an alacrity that narrowed his eyes suspiciously on her face.

'That's all?'

'Of course. What else could it be?' Had Lesli told him? —but his next words vetoed that idea.

'It's a combination of heat and lack of food,' he stated firmly, rising from the bed. 'As soon as I've showered and changed, I'll bring you a tray.'

Her head turned restlessly away on the pillow. 'I'm not hungry. Don't bother.'

'I'm going to bring you a tray,' he repeated grimly, 'and you'll eat the food on it if I have to spoonfeed it to you!'

He wheeled away from the bed and went back to his office bedroom without another word. Jinny watched him go with tremblingly compressed lips. His concern was genuine, she knew ... if only it was prompted by love instead of the prickly pride that would never let people believe he had starved her to death before discarding her!

The shower hissed for a surprisingly short time and the electric razor buzzed for only slightly longer before Bret was back in his room dressing. Jinny lay listening to the now familiar sounds of opening drawers, then clean shirt and trousers being taken from the closet. Sudden pain shafted through her. There would be so many things to miss when ...

She had already rinsed her tear-stained face and run a comb through her hair, which had dried to soft springiness round her face, when Bret tapped lightly on the door and came in bearing a tray which, with its four projecting legs, was obviously designed for bed use. He frowned when he saw her standing by the dressing table, his eyes flickering over the more decorous nightdress she had just had time to slip on.

'Would you mind getting back into bed and eating this before it falls flat?' he asked tersely.

'The tray?'

'No,' he returned with a sardonic smile. 'The omelette.'

He waited until she had climbed back into bed and settled herself with a pillow behind her before setting the tray carefully over her knees, seeming gratified when she gasped in amazement.

'Did *Lesli* do this?' The omelette lay in a half circle on the plate, light and fluffy as golden clouds in an evening sky, moistly ripe sliced tomatoes ranged artistically round it.

He surprised her by saying: 'No, I did. I'm not a lot of use in a kitchen, but there have been times when I've had to forage for myself. Anyway,' he sat beside her and adjusted the tray when his weight drew it down to one side, 'I didn't think you'd care for the concoction Lesli's creating for the evening meal.'

Jinny looked up and caught the wince on his darkly good-looking face and a giggle bubbled from her lips. Although she stifled it at once, appalled by her own inconsistency, her heart leapt when she saw an answering smile in his eyes. If only ... if only ... she lowered the black curtain of her lashes over eyes that were suddenly moist, picking up the fork beside her plate and pushing it blindly into the omelette.

'You don't have to stay,' she muttered, emotion thickening her voice to ungraciousness.

'I know,' he returned pleasantly, 'but I think I will. I'd hate to think of my culinary efforts being thrown out the window to the ranch hounds.'

'I *wouldn't*!' she lifted her head to say indignantly, and he took the fork from her hand, scooping up a section of the omelette and holding it to her lips.

'Then eat it!' he commanded so sternly that her mouth opened automatically to receive the fork. Twice more he lifted it to her mouth, then put it into her hand and got up to take a turn round the room as if sensing her embarrassment.

'I saw Endor on my way in,' he said, going to stand in front of the open window, his hands thrust into his pockets drawing the grey of his trousers tautly against his lean hips. 'His wounds seem to have healed, but he appears to have lost interest in what's going on around him.'

'Yes, I know,' she said in a low voice. 'I'm—going to set him free tomorrow.'

He swung round, surprised.

'You are? What made you decide that suddenly?'

'It's not sudden. I've always known I'd have to ... let him go.' Her eyes stayed on her plate, where only one tomato slice remained. 'It's wrong to try to keep something that can never belong to you.'

She heard him come slowly across to the bed and felt his eyes fixed on her bent head. Quietly, and with almost a note of regret in his voice, he said:

'Yes, that's true. I guess the same applies to people ... however much we want to hang on to them, if they want to be where there's happiness for them elsewhere, there's not much we can do, is there?'

'No,' whispered Jinny. 'It's useless trying to——' She broke off, biting her lip to keep back tears, but they filled her eyes anyway.

'There's no need for tears,' he said abruptly, bending to lift the tray with a swift, impatient movement. 'None of us particularly chooses where our ... affections will lie.'

He took the tray over to the dressing table and placed it there, his head bent for so long over the slightly ajar jewel drawer that Jinny had time to tissue away the tears which evidently annoyed him.

She heard the small drawer close with a decisive bang

and looked up in surprise when Bret strode back to her, his voice hopefully exuberant as he said:

'Jinny, we have to talk—no, I don't mean now,' he said impatiently when she shook her head. 'I have to go to Vancouver tomorrow morning. I'm taking Tim and Hank back, and there's some very important business I have to see to.'

His eyes glowed with eager enthusiasm and, although his lean body seemed to suddenly vibrate with an uncontrollable energy he sat beside her again, so close that the warmth from his body radiated to hers. If she had needed proof that he had understood that in giving up Endor she was also giving him up, it was there in abundance.

'Do you remember my telling you that our money problems would be solved in a few months?' he asked in a smiling rush of words. 'Well, I'm pretty sure tomorrow's the day I'll know for certain—something can always go wrong at the last minute, of course, but I don't expect it to.'

Tim and Hank had evidently given him a favourable report about their tests at Hillside, although why he should think something might go wrong at the last minute was beyond her—either the gold was there or it was not.

Bret seemed not to notice her lack of response, and continued more soberly: 'I'll have to be away overnight, Jinny, but when I get back the next day we'll talk and get everything straightened away. Meanwhile,' he rose and looked down intently into her eyes, 'get as much rest as you can. We have a lot to straighten away, Jinny.'

He surprised her again by leaning across her to press his lips lightly to hers just as Lesli opened the door and came in. Her elegantly shod feet slowed and came to a halt when she took in the scene at the bed, an angry frown descending like thunder between her eyes.

'Are you coming, Bret?' she asked sharply. 'Dinner's been ready for ten minutes, and it's going to be ruined if you don't come at once.'

'And my digestion will be ruined if I do,' Bret said *sotto*

voce to Jinny, but gave Lesli a flashing smile as he straightened, saying in his normal voice: 'I'll be right there.'

Scarcely glancing at Jinny, Lesli went to hold the door
open until he moved away from the bed and picked up the
tray from the dressing table.

'I'll see you the day after tomorrow,' he paused to say,
and followed Lesli from the room without waiting for a
reply from Jinny.

She lay with her eyes on the door for a long time after
they left. Would she really be doing Bret a favour in handing him over to Lesli? It seemed incredible, and somehow
distasteful, that a man of his calibre should subvert that
part of his nature which was most attractive to women—the
aggressively masculine side of him—to the possessive
domination of Lesli.

But then, she reflected wryly, Bret was bound by the
unbreakable tie of an early love just as much as she herself
was. Nothing, not even his ruthless self-seeking exploitation
of her grandfather, could break that bond.

As if verifying the fact, she touched her lips lightly with
her fingers. There had been more of gratitude than passion
in the kiss he had placed there ... a reward for little Jinny,
who had finally seen reason.

No, she wouldn't be here when Bret came back to
'straighten things away'. By the time he returned, she
would be far from Valley Ranch.

CHAPTER TEN

JINNY waited the next morning until she heard the plane
take off with a sudden surge of vibrating power before she
went along to the kitchen. She had been dressed for what
seemed hours, but the painful possibility of seeing Bret

again had confined her to the bedroom, and he had not come there. She was glad he hadn't. Even the sound of his cheerful whistling in the bathroom while he showered and shaved had sent a piercing bolt of pain through her.

Pouring herself some coffee from the still warm pot, she carried it over to the table and sat looking out on the patio where the petunias she had planted raised happy faces to the morning sun. Who would take care of them when she had gone? No one, probably. They would fade away and die from lack of attention. Just as she herself would fade away from Valley Ranch, but not to die. She had her baby ... Bret's baby ... to live for.

The thought brought such a surge of warm tenderness that Jinny could even feel a twinge of compassion for Lesli, who would never know the joy of bearing the child of the man she loved. At least on that point, Lesli and Bret were in agreement!

A cloud darkened the sky and cast a shadow over the patio. At last the heatwave was breaking, she thought thankfully, frowning when she recalled that after today it wouldn't matter one way or the other to her.

Bret had been more than generous with housekeeping money and, although she hated to take even that from him, she must have enough to support herself and prepare for the baby's birth in Vancouver. Together with the small amount she had left from the sale of Hillside cattle, it should be enough to see her through until she was in a position to take a job of some kind. Perhaps as housekeeper on a ranch somewhere, where her child would be welcome too.

After forcing herself to swallow a lightly boiled egg and washing it down with more coffee, she did the dishes left over from Lesli's and the three men's breakfasts by hand, glad of a task that would occupy her restless hands. As soon as she had finished that, she went along to the twin-bedded room Tim and Hank had shared and stripped the beds, putting the sheets in the washing machine while she remade the beds with fresh linen. Concentrating on ordinary household tasks kept her mind away from the dangers of dwelling on her turbulent emotions, but at last she had to admit that the house was clean and tidy from front porch to back door.

Much more difficult was the packing of the things she would take with her. Choosing became so hard that she at last pulled everything from the hangers and stuffed them into two suitcases, her throat tight with unshed tears as she turned to the dressing-table drawers. Underwear, tights and nightdresses were all swept into the cases, but she hesitated when she came to the last small drawer with its compartments for jewellery.

There in the middle section at the front lay her engagement ring, mocking in its diamond brilliance, and beside it was the cigar wrapper Bret had placed on her right hand at first. Somehow the simple band had come to symbolise much more than the expensive ring, and looking at it now she saw again Bret's laughing eyes as he slid it on to her finger. Compressing her lips to tear-defying tightness, she picked up the cigar band and left the ring in the drawer. Bret might want to give it to Lesli to add to the glittering gems already on her fingers.

She closed the suitcases and carried them one by one to the front door, dismayed by their heaviness. But the taxi driver would load them on to his car, and in his turn the long-distance bus driver would do the same. Glancing at her watch, she was surprised to see that the hands stood at a few minutes before two. There was time before the bus left at four, however, to say goodbye to Careen and Fitz and set Endor free.

Time, too, for instant coffee and a sandwich. Not that food appealed to her at that moment, but there might be long hours before she could eat again, and the baby must receive nourishment even if his mother gagged at the thought. Since her dream yesterday, she had come to think of the baby as a boy, one who would be the image of his father.

'Jinny? You there?'

As was the custom at Valley Ranch, Frank Milner gave a brief knock on the kitchen door and walked in, taking off his hat and mopping his brow as he did so.

'Yes, I'm here, Frank. Did you want something?'

'Just to see that you're okay,' he said, his eyes creasing in a grin. 'I see you are—looking very fancy too.' His gaze went admiringly over her white trouser suit belted snugly at the waist. 'I'm just going down with the boys to fix that roof on the lean-to down the Valley—Bret wants the hay kept dry in there, and it looks as if we're in for a dilly of a storm. Bret asked me to look in on you—said you hadn't been feeling up to scratch.'

'No, I—but I'm fine now. I was just going down to see the horses and . . . set the eagle free.'

Frank's smile broadened. 'That's news I'm glad to hear, Jinny. But you're not going down there like that, are you?' His eyes travelled again over her white suit.

Her cheeks coloured, and she said hesitantly: 'Frank, I—I'm going away for a while, and . . . would you take care of Careen and Fitz for me?'

Frank's smile faded, his eyes taking on a sober look as he asked quietly: 'You're going away without telling Bret?'

She nodded, turning back to the counter where she had been making the sandwich. 'He'll understand.'

'Well, I don't!'

Jinny swung round in surprise, the knife she had picked up still in her hand. She had never seen Frank so agitated.

'Do you think it's fair to run off the minute a man turns his back?' he demanded with gruff harshness. 'That's what happened to me, and I can tell you it's hell coming into a house when the reason for you coming isn't there any more! You can't do that to Bret, Jinny—go off and leave him alone.'

She turned away and bent over the half-made sandwich, biting her lip to control its trembling before saying huskily: 'He won't be alone, Frank.'

'Oh.' A wealth of understanding was in that one word, and Jinny resisted a hysterical desire to throw herself into Frank's broad arms and sob her heart out.

'I'm sorry, Jinny, I—didn't know. It's your sister, I guess. I thought it was strange the way she hung on here ... but, by God, Bret should have his hide whipped, and I'm not afraid to do it!'

'No, Frank! It's not his fault, it's—just one of those things nobody can help. Please don't say anything about it to Bret. I don't want him to know I've told you.'

Frank's jaw tensed menacingly, then his eyes softened as he looked at her drooping shoulders. 'All right,' he nodded, 'if that's what you want.'

'And you'll take care of the horses for me?'

'They'll have all the care they'll take—though if I know them, that won't be much. They're used to you, Jinny.'

'They'll manage without me,' she said with a staunchness she was far from feeling. 'Thanks, Frank.'

'You're sure you'll be all right?' His brown eyes looked piercingly into hers.

'Yes—yes, everything's fixed up,' she lied, wishing now that he would go and leave her alone.

As if sensing this he patted her awkwardly on the shoulder and muttered a gruff: 'Goodbye, Jinny. I...' He stumped out without finishing whatever it was he wanted to say, and Jinny went to push the sandwich dispiritedly away and pick up the cooled coffee, taking it over to the table and collapsing into a chair.

A sudden gust of wind shook the windows and drew her eyes outside to where the men were leaving in a pick-up truck. The sky held very little blue now, and heavy grey clouds rolled in across the mountains to obscure even that. Trees waved and began to bend in the wind, straw was driven from the stables to dance wildly across the lawn and round the patio, and when the windows shook again with renewed vigour Jinny jumped up and went round the house closing them against the certain storm to come.

A few minutes later she screwed up her eyes against the flying dust and hurried across to the stables. The horses further along the block were more concerned about the storm than were the stoical Careen and Fitz, and Jinny went along patting each one reassuringly and murmuring the unintelligible words that soothed them.

Careen's darkly soft eyes looked wistfully at her, hoping for the exercise Jinny had not given them for two days past, but Fitz stared in his proud masculine manner for only a moment before returning to the hay rack beside him. Jinny smiled ruefully as she gave his rump a farewell pat. Nothing would ever bother Fitz.

The mare, however, was different. She had been with Denis O'Brien before Jinny was born, and was the first horse the small orphaned child ever sat upon. Careen had been her constant friend and companion since that day.

As if sensing her young mistress's distress, the old mare nuzzled her velvety lips against her neck and Jinny, disregarding the snow white of her suit, threw her arms round the smooth neck and buried her face in its silky warmth.

'I'll come back one day,' she promised through blinding tears. 'We'll all be together again at Hillside—somehow.'

Unable to bear a more prolonged parting, Jinny kissed the mare between the eyes and rushed from the stable, hearing Careen's gentle snicker of regret as she closed the door.

'One day,' she told herself with gritted teeth as she made her way towards Endor's cage, 'I *will* come back to Hillside.'

If Lesli was right—and there was no reason to think she was not a lot more conversant with Bret's plans than Jinny had ever been—then his main interest still lay in his plane business, not the ranch. Had his seeming eagerness to develop Valley Ranch on modern lines been a cover-up for his real intention of subsidising and enlarging his fleet of planes? When he had come back to the Valley for his father's funeral, surprised that the old man had left the ranch to him, there had been no doubts in his mind that he would sell to the cattle company. It was only after he had talked with her grandfather ... Had Pop told him something about the gold, something he had never divulged to anyone else?

Jinny sighed. Whatever the answer to those questions were, they were unimportant now. Strangely, she was beginning to realise that it was the dream of gold that had been important to her grandfather and, in a lesser way, to herself—not the realisation of that dream.

In any case, even if Bret retained control of Valley Ranch, it was unlikely Lesli would agree to living there, far from the city action she loved. And after Bret's meek submission to her command the evening before, it was hard to visualise him making a strong demand of his own where Lesli was concerned. If all that was true, that would leave Jinny free to come back and live with her child on her half of Hillside ...

She stopped suddenly and bit her lip. If the will Lesli had found yesterday was valid, Hillside belonged to Bret! Her grandfather had stipulated that she and Bret should marry, but there was no clause stating that they must remain married for Bret to inherit.

'Oh, Pop!' she cried silently as her feet moved slowly on again. 'Why did you have to do things that way? Now I can never come back to Hillside!'

It was as she approached Endor's cage that she realised the wind had dropped, leaving an eerie quietness over the deserted ranch. Massed inky blue clouds misted the mountain tops and cast a darkening pall over the broad Valley with its open meadows, visible now for only a few hundred yards.

Although the air was still stickily humid, Jinny gave an involuntary shiver, thankful in an abstract way that Bret would not be flying today. Not for several days, she calculated with a quick glance at the mountains. By the time he was able to get back to the ranch, she would be far away in the anonymity of the city. Later, she would contact Karen and ask her permission to use that address for the necessary divorce papers, and then she would be free to make a new life for herself and her child. Maybe it would be best, after all, if Hillside and Gold Valley were left far behind them.

A soft exclamation broke from her lips when she came up to Endor's cage and saw the once proud king of birds hunched miserably on the wooden spar Bret had put across the cage for him. Around the dejected eagle lay the untouched offerings of mice from the stable cats, and his yellow-gold eyes, when he opened them, held a lacklustre glaze.

'Oh, Endor,' she breathed, 'I'm sorry.'

Guilt washed over her when she realised that her own selfish need to hold on to this symbol of a happier life had reduced him to the sorry state he was now in. The parallel between Endor, kept against his will from the freedom he needed to survive, and Bret, locked into a marriage he no longer needed, was too obvious to miss.

With trembling fingers, Jinny worked at the fastenings on the cage door and at last stood back as it swung open.

'Come on, Endor, you can go back to where you want to be,' she said softly, feeling rewarded when his eyes took on a more alert look at the sound of her voice. In another moment, she had stepped away from the entrance, and he was approaching it with cautious hops as if unable to believe that the freedom he craved was to be his at last.

A sudden flash of lightning and the ensuing roll of thunder reverberating along the Valley were the incentive he needed to take his last steps to release from the hated cage, but he paused again some yards from it and tested his wings experimentally.

'Please—let him be able to fly,' Jinny prayed silently, and as if in answer Endor croaked and spread his wings again, working up enough momentum to take him to the lowest branch of a nearby cottonwood tree, where he settled momentarily to look back at Jinny with implacably fierce eyes.

Tears stung her eyes then as he spread his wings again and lifted strongly into the sky, climbing with such speed that in seconds he was a mere ball against the dark clouds, a minute fragment buffeted by the high crosswinds that were even fiercer today because of the storm.

The first heavy drops of warm rain fell on Jinny's up-raised face, and she said at last silent farewell to Endor before turning towards the house, quickening her pace as the rain began to thud into the dry ground. Her last ties to Gold Valley had been severed, and now there was only the actual physical leavetaking. She was glad the storm had broken that day ... it would have been harder to leave a sundrenched, heartachingly familiar Valley.

Her foot stumbled over a tuft of grass in the pasture as her head lifted suddenly, her eyes straining towards the lowering sky. The pulsing throb of a plane's engine came again, though the machine itself was hidden from view above the clouds. Bret! Her feet began to move with increasing speed across the grass as her thoughts went chaotically to her readied suitcases on the front porch. Could she load them into the Stafford car, as she still thought of it, and be on her way before Bret and Lesli had time to reach the house? She broke into a run, her thoughts flying faster than her feet. What had possessed Bret to fly on a day like this? His office must be supplied with up-to-the-minute weather reports, so ignorance was no excuse for flying into the worst storm of the year in the enclosed Valley.

The plane's noise grew loud overhead, then receded down the Valley. Bret would be turning down there for his run-in to the landing strip. Perhaps she would have time after all, she thought, sprinting the last few yards to the log fence separating the pasture from the ranch buildings, already hearing the increasing loudness of the returning plane, when her foot hit the lowest rail.

She was astride the top rail when she heard the first heart-stopping silence of the engine, then the gathering roar as it sprang to life again. Panting, she straddled the rail and forgot her reason for hurrying when the engine spluttered off into silence again. Open-mouthed, she scanned the heavy clouds in the direction from which the plane's last spurt of life had come, her heart seeming suspended with her breath.

Then, closer than she expected and looking much larger than normal, the white and red plane plunged out of the clouds, ominous silence trailing its path as it descended quickly—too quickly—towards the sheer-faced mountain beyond the landing strip.

Paralysed, Jinny widened her eyes in horror as the inevitable crash drew closer. Like a slow-motion film, the plane blended with the rocky side of the mountain and she saw the left wing sail into the air and fall with a lazy motion seconds before the crackling sound reached her.

'Bret!'

Scarcely realising that the hoarse scream came from her own parched throat, Jinny leapt from the fence and ran with feet that scarcely touched the ground towards the crippled plane which was lodged now at a precarious angle further along the yellowed rock side of the mountain.

Across the landing strip she flew, the only sound in the rain-soaked silence her own laboured sobs. 'Bret! Oh, Bret, please...' Desperate prayers scurried through her mind, bargaining prayers that if God let Bret live she would never ask Him for one other thing in her life...

She heard Lesli's screams long before she had covered the grassy lower slopes of the mountain, weird unearthly screams that curdled her blood and sent her feet moving faster up the gradually increasing rockiness of the incline. She found Lesli's writhing body some distance below the plane where she had fallen in an obvious attempt to flee from the crash. Kneeling beside her sister, her breast heaving from the superhuman run across to the mountain, Jinny gasped:

'Lesli? Are you hurt? Lesli! Stop screaming and listen!'

Lesli's movements stopped as her eyes focused on Jinny's face, and she reached up with clutching fingers, rain washing over her own grey face.

'Jinny! Oh, Jinny—it was awful! I thought I was going to—die!'

A cursory glance assuring her that Lesli had not been physically damaged in the crash, Jinny leaned over her and asked urgently:

'Lesli, what about Bret? Where is he?'

Renewed screams brought swift action from Jinny's hand. Without thinking, she slapped Lesli smartly on each side of her face, seeing the shocked surprise and then the soft sobbing as hysteria left her.

'He's—in the plane, hurt. Can't get—out.'

Jinny looked with horrified eyes at her bedraggled sister. Bret trapped in the plane that was lodged so precariously above them on a ledge scarcely wide enough to take both wheels?

'Listen, Lesli,' she squatted down in front of her, looking urgently into her face. 'You'll have to go for help. Go back to the ranch as fast as you can and phone Mike or whoever else is at the R.C.M.P. Station. Tell him what's happened, that we need help in a hurry . . . and the doctor for Bret.'

Please let there still be a need for the doctor, she prayed silently, casting an upward glance through the falling rain to the frighteningly narrow ledge.

'You can't go up there,' Lesli shouted, correctly inter-
preting that look. 'That plane's going to slide off any minute
and crash down there!' Her panicked eyes went to the
jumbled rocks lying underneath the ledge, and Jinny knew
she was right. The machine would break to pieces down
there, and everything in it.

'Hurry!' she said urgently, getting to her feet and pulling Lesli with her. 'Bret's life depends on you.'

She watched while Lesli, with a last frightened look over
her shoulder, slithered down the slope and reached the
sodden flat, then went in a stumbling half-run towards the
buildings. Then, her heart and eyes filled with misgiving,
she herself climbed up the steeper incline to the crippled
plane, getting on to her hands and knees for the last few
yards. Dead or alive, she couldn't let Bret plunge down the
mountainside to oblivion.

Ignoring the stones that cut into her knees through the
light material of her slacks, she reached the ledge and edged
along it until the plane's door was directly above her.
Cautiously, she raised herself to a standing position and
forced her eyes to the interior, her heart lurching painfully
when she saw Bret's inert figure slumped in the pilot's seat,
his head fallen to one shoulder, arms hanging loosely by his
sides. Blood oozed from a triangular cut on his forehead,
running down to mat thickly in the dark hair over his
temple. The shattered windscreen in front of him bore mute
testimony to the origin of the wound.

Her eyes flew back to his drained face when a low groan
came from him. He was alive! Alive! She swung herself up
into the cockpit, scarcely noticing the ominous shifting of
the plane's body beneath her as she crawled across the passenger seat and raised Bret's head to lean in an upright
position against the seat back. Her fingers searched for the
rain-soaked paper tissue in the pocket of her suit, and she
dabbed gently at the wound on his brow, gladness surging
through her when his lids fluttered and opened.

'Jinny?' His breath was a mere flutter through his lips. 'What—what——?'

'It's all right, Bret,' she soothed. 'There was a crash, but we'll get you out.'

'Crash?' His eyes wandered round the cockpit, then filled with horror. 'Lesli! What happened to——?'

'She's okay,' Jinny answered briefly, knowing there would be time later for hurt that his first thought had been for the woman who had abandoned him to his fate. 'Put your arm over my shoulders and I'll help you out.'

His hand had begun to lift when the plane gave a sickening sideways lurch and his fingers tightened with surprising strength on her arm before pushing her away.

'Get out of here, Jinny!' he said, hoarsely urgent. 'She ... won't hold much ... longer.'

'Not without you.' She leaned across to slide her arms under his and heave against his solid weight, finding it immovable and panting at last: 'Can't you help yourself at all?'

'I don't seem to be able to get my foot out from under the pedal,' he said quietly, and her eyes swivelled sharply to the foot controls, nausea rising bitterly to her throat when she saw the unnatural angle of his leg and black-shoed foot wedged tightly under the pedal. Her own sickness was reflected in his pain-filled eyes when she turned back to him.

'Bret, I have to do something—there *must* be something——'

His mouth clamped into a tight white line as the plane shifted again. 'There's just one thing you can do—get the hell out of here! Now!'

Before she realised what was happening, he had propelled her with surprising force across the passenger seat and poised her in the doorway so that she had no choice but to jump to the ground. Gravel pierced her hands and knees, but she didn't feel it in her fright at seeing a sheet of muddy rainwater cascading down the rocks and flowing

across the ledge, loosening the gravel under the plane's
thick black wheels. Even as she watched, hypnotised, the
delicately balanced outer wheel slid and half disappeared
over the ledge, leaving the plane tilted at an even more
precarious angle.

'Bret!'

The scream was torn from her throat as she stretched up
to the open door. Bret had fallen across the passenger seat
after pushing her out, and lay with such white-faced stillness that Jinny sobbed helplessly, her head supported
against her sodden arm.

'Jinny?'

She looked up, her vision blurred with tears and rain,
and saw that his eyes were partly open and focused on her.
His voice was no more than a series of gasps when he said:

'Lesli said ... is it—true? ... Baby...'

Her breath caught on a sob. With his eyes so intent on
her, all thoughts of denial fled from her mind. A man who
knew that instant death could come with the next shift of a
crippled machine deserved to know that his child would
survive him.

'Yes, Bret. It's true.'

He continued to stare at her while rain thudded and
hissed round them, then his lips moved again.

'I'm ... sorry, Jinny. I ... didn't want...'

His eyes closed as he relaxed into unconsciousness again,
and Jinny pulled away from the plane, her breath held in
suspension as she gazed disbelievingly at him. Even now, in
the face of disaster, he had reiterated his aversion to children ... to his own child.

The gurgle of water from behind brought her head round
dazedly to see that rain was cascading down the sheer rock-
face and settling in a pool at the wheel's base. Her shocked
hurt was pushed away immediately, and she glanced round
with desperate eyes, seeing a large oval rock part-way up a
less sheer section of the slope. If she could somehow roll

that down and wedge it against the wheel . . .

Almost before the thought had formed, she was scrambling up to the rock. Rain had loosened it, too, and it was comparatively easy to start it on its downward roll, but her heart stopped beating as she watched it gather speed and rush towards the ledge, threatening to crash against the far wheel and accomplish the very thing she was trying to avoid.

She let out her breath cautiously when the huge stone rolled to a stop a scant foot away from the wheel, and in another few seconds she was down beside it, inching its dead weight towards the wheel base. With a superhuman strength born of panic, the boulder was moved to settle at last as a wedge against the side back of the wheel.

Dizziness overtook her as she straightened, but a glance at Bret's white face galvanised her into action again and she swung herself back up to the cockpit. A faint moan from his lips convincing her that she could not afford to wait for the help that was coming, her eyes went down to the jammed pedal against Bret's foot. If she could find something to prise it up with, a tool of some sort . . . hadn't she noticed a canvas bag of tools behind Bret's seat on the two occasions she had flown with him?

Crawling between the two seats, she sobbed her relief when her groping fingers encountered the rough canvas. Opening the bag with feverish fingers, she pulled out a tool shaped like a chisel and a small hammer. It would be difficult to work in such a cramped space, but another motion of the undercarriage lent speed to her fingers as they wedged the chisel under the pedal and struck it sharply upwards with the hammer.

Nothing happened. Although she struck it again and again, the pedal remained as firmly stuck as before, and she paused, sobs strangling her as she realised how hopeless her efforts had been. She couldn't save Bret . . . probably not even herself. Pain knifed across her back, bringing an acrid nausea into her throat. At least she would die with Bret, although she had not been able to live with him ...

The rain had stopped suddenly, so that the audible click of the pedal releasing itself came loudly to her ears. For long moments she stared down at it as if disbelieving the evidence of her eyes. Bret's foot was free! Another faint groan from him set her into automatic action. Gritting her teeth, she grasped his ankle and eased his foot from under the pedal before turning to look helplessly at his six-foot-plus frame.

She slid her arms under his and, using every ounce of the stamina she had left, succeeded in moving him only an inch or two towards the door. Bitter frustration made her pound her fists softly against his chest, and then with a sob she laid her head there, hearing the weak but steady rhythm of his heart under her ear. But of what use was it that his heart still beat if ...

Her head lifted when voices came from the slope outside. Relief flooded her body, relaxing her so that her head fell back to Bret's chest. Mike must have responded to Lesli's call for help in record time!

But it was Frank's horror-stricken face that loomed up in the doorway, his eyes going rapidly from Jinny to Bret's white face. Behind him, the shocked expressions of several ranch hands came and went with frightening rapidity. She heard a jumble of male voices, then rough hands grasping and pulling her.

'Bret——'

'We'll get him out, Jinny,' Frank's stark voice answered, and she felt herself being handed back to other strong arms.

Cradled against the unknown shoulder, Jinny saw the mountain spin dizzily over them ... toppling ... falling on them. The sound of a terrifying crash echoed through her brain as the rocks covered her with darkness ...

'Jinny? Jinny?'

Doctor Barker's face swam before her eyes, familiar yet unreal in its shifting pattern. Was Pop ill again? But why was she sleeping when Pop needed her?

'Come on, Jinny, come back now.'

Back? Back from where? She had been away . . . yes, she had been in Vancouver . . . cars, hundreds of cars far below . . . Bret's smiling face . . . a ring . . . strong brown hands on a plane's wheel . . .

She started up suddenly. '*Bret!*'

'He's all right, Jinny,' the doctor said soothingly. 'He has a fractured leg and a cut on the head, but he's going to be okay.'

Jinny settled back again on the pillows, her body feeling light and untrammelled . . . she gasped and shot forward again. 'My—baby?'

The answer was clear to her in the doctor's sad eyes even before he said: 'I'm sorry, Jinny. It wasn't possible to save the baby. If it's any consolation to you, your courage in saving the baby's father makes it possible for you and Bret to have other children.'

'No,' she said quietly, subsiding rigidly against the pillows. 'There won't be any others.'

'Of course there will,' Doctor Barker said heartily, patting her hand. 'You're a healthy young couple, there's no reason why——'

'There's a very good reason,' she said coldly, turning her head away to stare with hard eyes at the square of window beyond the bed. 'Divorced couples don't usually have children.'

'*What?*' The doctor's nut brown eyes widened in astonishment. 'That's not what I understood from Bret.'

She laughed shortly. 'I don't suppose it was! My husband's a very proud man, doctor. He wouldn't want anyone to think he didn't appreciate that I helped save his life.'

'I think you have it all wrong, Jinny,' he said gently. 'If ever I saw a husband concerned about his wife——'

'No, *you* have it all wrong, doctor.' She leaned up on her elbows and looked directly into his eyes. 'Do you know what he said when I told him it was true I was having his child? He said...' she paused to draw a difficult breath, '... he said "I'm sorry!" And that was when he thought he was about to *die*!'

He looked incredulously into the hard dryness of her eyes for a moment, then put her back gently on the pillow. 'I'm going to give you something to calm you down, Jinny. We'll talk about this again later.'

'I don't want to see or hear anything about my husband,' she said distinctly when he came back from the side of the room to push a needle into her arm.

'All right, Jinny, if that's what you want,' he said soothingly.

CHAPTER ELEVEN

EARLY October sunshine shafted through the long, high windows of the play-school, lighting Jinny's hair to blue-black brilliance as she moved among the young children who were absorbed in the finger painting task she had set them.

'Not like that, Bobby,' she said, leaning over the bench where a five-year-old slashed poster paints across the desk as well as the paper. 'Keep it on the paper. What are you drawing?'

'It's my house, and my mommy,' he said, raising injured eyes to hers. 'Can't you tell?'

'Oh, yes,' she lied, 'I see now, but keep it on the paper, Bobby—you can't take the table home to show your mother, can you?'

He grinned, and her heart swelled in her breast as she

moved on. Her own child would have looked like Bobby—grey eyes, dark hair, sturdy little body.

But she was doing what she had promised herself never to do—searching the faces and personalities of the children under her care for likenesses to the child she had lost.

Perhaps she was indulging her fancies particularly today, knowing she would be seeing Karen and Tom that night for the first time since she had left Gold Valley three months before. Although in the strictest sense, she had not returned to the Valley after the plane crash. Mike had been more than helpful when he knew the circumstances, taking time to pick up her suitcases from Valley Ranch although he himself was leaving the Valley for his new post earlier than expected. It was Mike, too, who had put her on the plane to Vancouver when she was released from the hospital, Mike who had accepted her quietly spoken rejection of him as a husband with understanding grace . . .

Now she wondered if it had been a wise move to accept Karen's invitation to dinner. Jinny's purpose in calling her the day before had been to facilitate Bret's inevitable seeking for a divorce, and Karen, after her initial shock at hearing Jinny's voice, had agreed readily to using her own address as a mailing centre. Her urgings for Jinny to come and see them had pierced the hurtful shell of loneliness she had surrounded herself with, and she had agreed to join them for a meal.

Sighing, Jinny looked at the clock above the door. 'All right, children, you can get ready to go home now. Tidy everything away—and you can take your pictures home.'

Home for her, unlike the children whose mothers came to pick them up and take them back to a happy family unit, was a two-room apartment not far from the school. The converted older house faced on to a well-tended park, but the carefully nurtured shrubs and sculptured grass slopes were a long way from Gold Valley's peaks and rugged grandeur. Especially when, as now, a whole weekend stretched in front of her.

A taxi deposited her promptly at seven in front of the neatly laid out lawns in front of Karen and Tom's house, and Karen was beaming in the doorway when Jinny walked up the cement path towards it.

'Jinny! I can't tell you how glad I am to see you! We'd no idea you were in the city ... we thought——'

Radiant in a pale blue loose dress, Karen drew Jinny into the house and cast a concerned eye over her too-thin body in close-fitting navy dress.

'You look well, Karen,' Jinny said quietly, stifling her stab of envy at the fair girl's obvious happiness in her pregnancy when Tom appeared from the living room.

'Good to see you, Jinny,' he said easily, coming over to hug her slight frame with his bear-like arms. 'We missed you.'

Jinny's hard-won equilibrium faltered under the warm acceptance of his smile and Karen, her own eyes suspiciously misty, ushered them both into the living room.

To Jinny's relief, no mention was made of Bret or the accident, Tom and Karen treating her simply as an old friend they had not seen for some time, and gradually she relaxed. She told them what she was doing, but not where, and Karen seemed interested in her stories about the children she supervised.

They had almost finished dinner when the telephone rang in the hall, and Karen exchanged a quick glance with Tom.

'I'll get it,' she said, putting her napkin beside her plate as she rose and excused herself to Jinny.

'Most likely somebody from one of the clubs she's joined since she stopped working for——' Tom broke off abruptly, his fair-skinned face reddening.

'It's all right, Tom,' Jinny said quietly. 'You work for Bret, and he's your friend, it's only natural you should mention him.' She dropped her eyes to the fork she twisted between slender fingers. 'How is he? Has he recovered from the accident?'

Tom looked at her oddly. 'Physically he's fine—the leg is mending pretty well, but——'

Karen's voice carried clearly through the open door. 'Well, I'm sorry, but there's nothing I can do to help. I know nothing about horses, and my husband knows even less ... Yes, Bret left a number where he could be reached, but—What? It's Jinny's horse you're worried about? ... No, there's no way I can get in touch with her, and even if I could——'

Jinny had been drawn like a magnet to Karen's side, doubt mingling with concern in her eyes as she signalled that she would speak. It seemed too much of a coincidence that someone from Valley Ranch should call the very night she was here, but if there was something wrong with one of her horses, she wanted to know about it.

'Hold on a minute,' Karen said shortly, seeming irritated when she put her hand over the mouthpiece. 'It's a Frank Milner from Valley Ranch—he's worried about a horse he says belongs to you—Katreen, or——'

'Careen!' Jinny exclaimed, her brow furrowing with anxiety but checking the hand she held out for the receiver. 'You're sure it's Frank at the other end, not——?'

'I swear to you it's not Bret, Jinny,' Karen said with clear-eyed candour. 'He went to Europe, you know, and ...'

'Oh, yes. I'd forgotten about that.' Jinny took the receiver without further hesitation and said: 'Frank? It's Jinny. What's wrong with Careen?'

'Jinny! It's sure good to hear your voice again,' Frank's slow but delighted drawl came across the wire. 'I didn't think I'd be lucky enough to——'

'What about Careen, Frank?'

'Well, she's in a pretty bad way, Jinny. She's been fretting for you ever since you ... but now she won't even eat, and I'd hate to see a fine horse like her go before her time.

Is there any way you can get down here, even for just a little while? It might make quite a difference to her.'

'No, I—I couldn't come down there, Frank. You know why.'

Jinny heard Tom say something to Karen in the background and Frank's words became a muffled blur in her ear.

Karen laid a hand on her arm and whispered: 'Tom says he'll take you down there tomorrow. He can drop you off on his way up north to deliver some supplies and pick you up on the way back. You'd have two or three hours there.'

'Just a minute, Frank,' said Jinny, her throat suddenly dry. 'Tom, I—I don't think I could go in a plane again after...'

'Sure you can,' Tom said confidently, coming to stand near her. 'I'm a very good pilot, if I say so myself.'

'So was Bret,' Jinny said in a whisper, and heard a swift intake of breath at the other end of the line. Evidently Frank hadn't forgotten that afternoon on the mountain slope either.

'Bret took the only foolish risk I've known him to take when he flew into the Valley that day in that kind of weather,' said Tom in a terse voice. 'I'm not going to be in that kind of hurry to get there. I promise I won't even take off if there's the slightest chance of bad weather.'

Torn between her dread of the flight and concern for Careen, Jinny hesitated for only a moment, then nodded.

'All right, Tom, I'll go.'

'Relax, Jinny,' Tom's voice came above the noise of the engine, and he patted her knee in a brief, comforting gesture. 'It's a beautiful day for flying.'

Jinny realised then that her hands were clenched whitely in her lap, her jaw stiff with tension, and she made a conscious effort to relax as Tom had advised. Patting the knees of nervous female passengers must be a thing with small plane pilots, she thought wryly, remembering her first flight with Bret and the reassuring squeeze from his capable brown fingers.

Her mind skirted quickly round that dangerous subject. It was only her proximity to Valley Ranch, which she had thought never to see again, that had opened a crack in her stiffly held resolve never to think of Bret as he had been in his better moments. Those moments had been few and far between in their short marriage. But she could have forgiven him Lesli, and even his materialistic motive for marrying herself, and gone on to make a reasonably contented life for herself and ...

She turned her head sharply to look from the side window at the passing mountains where snow still clung to the higher crevices. She could have forgiven Bret anything except his repudiation of his child even when he was at death's door. It had taken an especially hard man to leave those words of rejection with his pregnant wife, knowing it was almost certain he would never live himself to see that child. Now she realised that Bret was a man she had scarcely known. She had projected her early schoolgirl affection on to a man whose character was far removed from the boy she had loved, and she had paid a bitter price for that knowledge.

'About ten minutes now, Jinny,' Tom called cheerfully, and she nodded, forcing a smile. Her nerves were under icy control now.

She leaned forward a few minutes later when familiar landmarks began to appear beneath them—the Janssen ranch with its small huddle of buildings set on open prairie land, Potter's nurseries and the glittering rows of greenhouses, the Turner sawmills ...

Her stomach tightened as Gold Valley itself flashed by under them and up ahead, at the start of the Valley, the cluster of Valley Ranch buildings. The small plane banked over Hillside, and Jinny's eyes stung when she saw the squat outline of the house, the paddock and barn, nestled against the hill. Her eyes moved swiftly across the Hillside property, searching for signs of mine development, but everything looked the same as always. New corrals close to the lake caught her eye and disappeared behind them as they came down to land. Quarters for Bret's stock from Europe, she thought, faintly surprised that he had persisted in his cattle-buying spree. If Lesli had anything to do with it, it would be only a rich man's hobby to be indulged on occasional visits to the ranch.

Her eyes studiously avoided the site of Bret's crash as they bumped down on to the landing strip and drew to a halt. Tom's voice sounded suddenly loud in the silence.

'Well, we made it! It wasn't too bad, was it?'

'No,' she admitted, gathering up her slimline white handbag from the floor beside her. 'It was fine.'

Tom grinned and swung himself to the ground, coming round to help her down, his eyes going appreciatively over her trimly fitting pants suit of greenish-blue polyester. 'Can't remember when I've had a better looking passenger,' he joked, setting her on the ground.

'Wait till I tell Karen you said that!'

'If that's the way of it, I just might forget to pick you up on the way back!'

Jinny looked soberly up into his light blue eyes. 'No, don't do that, Tom. Can't you come up to the ranch with me?'

He shook his head and closed the passenger door. 'No, I have to push on now. But you'll be okay, Frank's around somewhere.'

She stood back and watched while he took off again into the cloudless blue sky, then turned and walked with slow footsteps across the grass bordering the landing strip, forcing from her mind the memory of the last time she had crossed there. Then, her feet had scarcely touched the ground as she sped across to the crippled plane ...

'Jinny!'

Her eyes lifted from the ground to see Frank at the end of the stable block, a smile wreathing his face. In another moment she was engulfed in his bear-like hug, resting with brief thankfulness on his broad shoulder.

'It's good to see you, Jinny,' he said huskily, holding her away while his eyes went over her. 'You're a lot thinner, though.'

'Some women pay a fortune to look like this,' she said with mock indignation, then her eyes grew serious. 'How is Careen?'

'Well, she seems a little better this morning,' he said, taking her arm as they moved towards the end section of the stables. 'It's as if she knew you were coming.'

The other horses snickered hopefully and blew through their noses when they passed, and Jinny looked eagerly at each one, realising how hungry she had been for the ranch life she loved. Her step quickened when they neared her own horses' stall.

'Oh, darlings,' she said softly, leaning over the half-door as her heart filled with tenderness at sight of the two closely aligned rumps. Quiet as her voice had been, Fitz pricked up his ears and moved restlessly to one side. But Jinny's concerned look was for Careen, who stood with dejectedly hanging head over her hay rack.

Murmuring in a tear-choked voice, Jinny undid the door and went in, sliding a hand along each chestnut back until she reached Careen's drooping head and clasped it to her breast.

'Oh, Frank,' she said with an anguished backward look at the sturdy ranch manager in the doorway, 'this is better?'

'Better than she has been, Jinny. She's missed you.'

Jinny caressed the velvety nose, still murmuring lovingly, and caught her breath when Careen's head lifted, her dark eyes looking blankly into Jinny's before recognition came to them. A tentative snicker was followed by a probing against the girl's neck and a sudden whinny as her scent penetrated the flaring nostrils . . .

It was a good half hour later when Frank reappeared at the stable door, smiling his approval at Careen's hungrily munching jaws.

'That reminds me,' he remarked conversationally, 'there's food up at the house for lunch.'

Jinny stiffened. 'No, I—I'm not hungry, Frank. I'll stay here until Tom gets back.'

'That might not be for hours yet,' Frank said stolidly. 'I made some sandwiches, but I confess I was looking forward to having you brew the coffee. Mine never tastes the way a woman's does.'

'Oh, Frank! What possible difference does it make if a man or a woman brews the coffee?'

'I don't know. All I know is that it tastes different when a woman does it.'

'All right,' she conceded with a sigh. Going into the kitchen at Valley Ranch would at least prove to herself that the past was behind her, buried in the oblivion it deserved.

'You will? Thanks, Jinny,' said Frank with a relieved smile. 'I'll come up to the house when I've rounded up Prince—he slipped through the gate when my back was turned.'

He turned and walked quickly away in the direction of a black stallion which was, she knew, the horse that was exclusively his. Giving a backward glance at Careen and Fitz, she fastened the door and made her way to the house, which lay as sleepy as a cat basking in the noonday sun.

Frank had seen that the lawns were kept green and trimmed while Bret was away, she thought, feeling the dampness from an earlier watering on her open-toed sandals as she stepped on to the flagstoned patio. Even the petunias she had planted . . . she stopped and stared down at the well-kept plants, still blooming profusely. A little care and attention was all they had needed to keep them happy, and from the looks of them, they had had more than a little of each.

The kitchen seemed cool and spacious when she went into it, and it was hard to picture herself there preparing meals for Bret, Lesli and herself. Apart from the plastic wrap covering sandwiches on the counter, it had the unused look of absent owners away on a vacation. Which of course was true, she reflected as she moved with remembered ease to the cupboard where the coffee pot was kept. Bret and Lesli were on a trip to Europe. Buying cattle.

She measured coffee into the pot and set it on the stove after filling it with water. The house was so quiet, she wished Frank had . . . Her head swivelled round to the door that led to the rest of the house. Beyond it came the sound that had alerted her ears to the presence of another being . . . an inhuman being . . . in the house with her. The odd sound increased in volume, and her eyes dilated with terror when the door slowly swung open.

'*You!*' she gasped, groping for support on the counter behind her, her face sheet white as she stared at the figure in the doorway.

'I'm sorry, Jinny, I didn't mean to scare you,' said Bret, moving with a pronounced limp towards her, his eyes going over her as if he sought to refresh a flagging memory.

'This . . .' she began thickly, '. . . this was a put-up job between all of you, wasn't it?' Her outraged eyes met his with dawning condemnation.

He stopped a few paces from her and though her eyes were clouded with anger, she saw the thinness of his face and gaunt figure, eyes that were sunk deeper than normal above prominent cheekbones.

'You could put it that way,' he agreed soberly. 'But don't blame the others. They did it because I asked them to.' He took another step towards her. 'Jinny, it was the only way to get you down here. I knew you wouldn't come unless it was for something you cared about.'

Her head reared back and she asked scornfully: 'And how did you manage to get Careen to act as if she was pining for me? Hollywood must be looking for animal trainers like you!'

His jaw tightened for a second, then relaxed. 'That much was true. She *has* been pining for you ...' his voice dropped to a lower note, '... we've all been——'

Her scornful laugh broke in on his words. 'I can imagine how that must have spoiled your trip to Europe with Lesli!' She saw his puzzled frown and went on: 'Or was that a fabrication too?'

'No, I went to Europe, but I haven't seen Lesli since the accident. I went because I thought—I thought you were with Mike Preston. You left at the same time as he did. I just got back three days ago, and I didn't know you were in the city ... on your own ... until Karen called me on Thursday. Jinny, I had to get you here,' he went on jerkily, 'I have to talk to you, explain ... you've never even given me the chance to thank you for—what you did.' His grey eyes were anguished as they stared into hers.

'You needn't have gone to all this trouble just for that,' she said briskly, picking up her bag from the counter. 'A letter to Karen's address would have sufficed.' She stepped towards the door, then turned back to add: 'Anyway, Bret, things even themselves out, don't they? An eye for an eye ... a life for a life!'

He flinched as if she had struck him and said stiffly: 'I'm—sorry, Jinny, about the baby. I didn't want——'

'You're saying it again!' she marvelled, her eyes flashing. 'You're using exactly the same words as you did up there. Don't you think I know by now that you didn't want the baby? But *I* wanted him, Bret, I——' Her voice filled with tears and she flung back to the door.

'For God's sake, what are you saying, Jinny?' He jerked her round to meet the stark grey of his eyes. 'If you had let me finish, you would have heard me say that I didn't want

my life in exchange for his—or hers! Don't you know how
often I've wished you had let me go and saved the child?'
he ended bitterly.

'But...' Her eyes searched his face with almost desperate hope. 'You've often said you didn't want—children.'

His other hand came up to grip her arm and he said
tersely: 'I didn't! How could I let my own children suffer
the way I had? Yet when ... Lesli told me just before the
crash ... everything seemed to fall into place. The cigar
band the night before...'

Her eyes were wide on his face. 'Cigar band?'

He gave her a look that verged on impatience and
dropped his hands from her as he turned to limp towards
the table. 'Yes, the cigar band—the one I gave you that
night before our wedding. I saw it in your jewel drawer the
evening you were ill. And even though you'd just been telling me how hopeless it was to hang on to you, I hoped when
I saw that...' His voice broke off into strained silence as
his hands took his weight on the table top.

'Bret, I...'

His face twisted into a tired grimace. 'Do you mind if we
sit down? There's a lot I want to say before Tom gets back,
and I can't stand on this leg for too long yet.'

'I'm sorry,' she said, guessing how much that admission
cost him. Almost against her own volition, she found herself
taking the seat opposite the one he had pulled out to settle
in with his leg stretched out beside the table. 'Is it—getting
better?'

'The leg is,' he answered briefly, 'but I can't say the
same for my temper. As a patient I'm not very patient.'

He leaned back in his chair and stared contemplatively at
her for so long that she felt colour rise in a warm wave from
her throat to cover her face, and her eyes shifted from his to
a spot below his white-sweatered chest. The sound of the
coffee pot bubbling over on the stove came as a welcome
relief and she rushed to lift the pot aside and turn off the

heat. Automatically, she poured coffee into a mug for him as well as for herself and carried it over to place it at his elbow.

'Thank you,' he said gravely, and she was conscious of his eyes on her while she mopped up the spills on the stove, then came back with her own coffee.

'Bret, why did you think I had gone with Mike?' she asked diffidently, more as a way of breaking the silence than making conversation.

He stared down into his coffee without answering for long moments, then lifted his head to say quietly, 'Because you both left at the same time, as far as I could gather when I got out of hospital, and ...' he sighed heavily, '... I'd heard you, the night of the party, telling him you were still in love with him.'

She gasped, her eyes widening. 'But I didn't tell him I was in love with *him*! I said I was still in love with——' She had rushed on without thinking, but now she stopped and bit her lip.

His hand reached across the table to cover hers in a bone-crushing hold, his voice hoarse when he said:

'Are you saying that—you weren't in love with Mike? That day at Hillside when I tried to tell you about the agreement I'd come to with Lesli you——'

'Oh, yes, Lesli,' she put in, a hard edge creeping round her voice. 'Can't you understand I didn't want to know anything about any agreements with Lesli?' she cried, lifting eyes darkened to midnight blue, pulling her hand away from his to push back the hair from her face. 'It was enough for me to see the first agreement at the airport when you brought her back!'

A muscle in his jaw contracted as he clenched his teeth. 'There was never any agreement in that sense as far as Lesli and I were concerned,' he bit off shortly. 'The only agreement I wanted from her was that she'd sell her half of Hillside, and she held out long enough, as you know.' His breath was expelled in a long sigh as he went on: 'That day at the airport—yes, she wanted to renew old acquaintance and misconstrued my efforts to comfort her, but I made it very clear to her that I was in love with my wife ... you! Can you understand how I felt when you acted like a frozen shrew after that? I couldn't believe that my sweet Jinny had changed into a vindictive woman overnight!'

Her eyes had not left his face, and now she cried agonisedly: 'Oh, Bret, why didn't you tell me?'

'Would you have believed me?' he asked bitterly, then shook his head. 'No. You'd made up your mind long before that Lesli and I had a far deeper relationship than ever existed. It was as if you *wanted* to believe that she and I belonged together. I thought the only way to convince you was to have her down here and show you she meant nothing to me, and hadn't for years.'

Shock riveted her eyes on the strained grey of his. What he had said was true ... she *had* assumed that his love for Lesli had been smouldering for years, not extinguished ... that Eddie's death, freeing Lesli, was all that was needed to rekindle the flames of the old love. Hadn't he——? Her gaze sharpened, and he said quietly:

'You still don't believe me, do you? What did you just think of?'

'You—you left Gold Valley the day after Lesli eloped with Eddie ...'

He made an impatient gesture with his hand. 'I didn't leave the Valley because of *Lesli*! That night, after you'd told me about it, I had the worst quarrel yet with my father. He always cared more about Jack, my older brother, than me. I didn't know how much he resented me until he said that night he wished I had been under that tractor instead of Jack. I couldn't stay in the house any longer after that.'

'Oh, Bret, I'm sorry,' she said brokenly, all her preconceived notions crumbling and failing to re-form into any pattern. 'I . . . didn't know.'

'No, you didn't know,' he agreed soberly. 'Maybe it was unfair of me to expect you to understand how I felt when I thought I'd finally found somebody real, somebody who cared more about the things that were important to me than what I could give her in return. That's why, I guess, I couldn't take it when you thought I'd take up with Lesli where you imagined I'd left off. Loving somebody means trusting them, I believed, and I couldn't bring myself to realise that you didn't love me at all until——'

'But I did, Bret,' she cried in a strangled sob. 'I've loved you since I was fourteen years old, but . . . Bret, what are you doing?'

'Something I should have done long ago,' he returned grimly, lifting her easily from her seat and swinging her up into his arms.

Even while she clasped her hands behind his neck, she whispered: 'Your leg.'

'That won't be a hindrance to what I have in mind,' he retorted, his jaw set determinedly as he carried her to the door and along the passage to the master bedroom.

'Bret?'

'Mmm?'

'What about . . . the gold . . . at Hillside?' she asked tentatively, and felt him stiffen against her, his head rising from the hollow of her shoulder.

'Jinny, I'm sorry, but there's no gold at Hillside.' He pulled himself up to a sitting position beside her, his arm muscles tensing. 'I'm sorry, honey,' he repeated, 'but your grandfather was wrong, as I'd always suspected.'

'Wrong?' she asked abstractedly, her hand coming up to brush through the thickest part of his hair.

'Yes—although not altogether wrong.' He leaned on one elbow and looked directly into her eyes. 'I didn't tell you at the time, but Tim and Hank are geologists. I knew you'd never completely given up that dream of gold, so I asked them to come down here and prove to you once and for all that it didn't exist.' His fingers, warmly light, touched her temple and his eyes darkened. 'They found there *is* a small seam, but it's further up the hillside, off O'Brien property. Your grandfather could never have developed it anyway, but it gave him something to dream about all those years— and that's important for any man.'

The corner of his mouth, lazily relaxed, turned up in a rueful half smile. 'He even had me help draw up a will leaving everything to me if you and I married, though...' his lips came down to rest lightly on her cheek, '... he knew I loved you. What else could we talk about between chess moves? But I guess it made him happy to feel he'd made provision for you.'

'Yes,' she agreed inaudibly against his ear. Obviously Lesli had not told him about finding that will, or the inter- pretation which had been put on it. Still...

'Bret, I don't understand—you said our money problems would be over, and I thought——'

'That's what I was rushing back to tell you the day of the crash!' He lifted his head again so that she saw the deep glow in his eyes. 'The airline sale had gone through finally, and——'

'You—*sold* your charter company?'

'Of course. I needed the money to expand the ranch. How else do you think I was able to buy the breed stock in Europe?' His voice dropped to a husky note. 'I'd planned on taking you with me, that ... maybe we'd have that honeymoon at last, but...' His fingers tightened at her throat. 'I almost went crazy when I thought you'd left with Mike Preston.'

'You could have come after me,' she suggested, a hint of reproach in her tone. 'If you——'

He sat up away from her and ran a hand through his hair.

'As far as I knew at the time, you were in love with him. All I had to go on was a cigar band I'd seen in your jewel drawer, and that could have meant everything or nothing ... women save things for different reasons, sometimes for no reason at all. Even though you took it with you when you left...' He frowned, his face falling back into its stern lines. 'And apart from that—you had lost your baby because of me.'

She swallowed painfully, her eyes dropping down over the taut leanness of his torso to rest on the sheet wrapped loosely round his hips.

'It was your baby too, Bret.'

'I know that,' he said quietly, and reached for her hand, crushing it under the hard pressure of his. 'My father was a hard man, Jinny, in some ways, especially after my mother died. I don't think he'd ever realised how much he depended on her, and—well, I won't go into all that now, but it left me with a prejudice against marriage and all it stood for.'

'Yet you ... asked Lesli.'

He gave a half shrug. 'Yes, once. But that was more in fun than seriousness, and I knew she'd turn me down. You know there'd been a few women in my life, Jinny, before I came back, but until I met you again and you gave me the rough side of your tongue about how I'd always loved the Valley, I'd never wanted any close attachments. You made me realise how much I'd missed the things that used to be important to me.' He released her hand and lay back on his own pillow, his eyes a dark grey as they stared up at the ceiling.

'That day in the plane, just before we were caught in the downwind, Lesli threw at me the news that you were pregnant.' His eyes met hers across the pillows. 'I knew we were about to crash, and all I could think of was you ... and the baby, that I'd never see him.' Rolling over so that his body lay alongside hers, hard and powerful where hers was soft and yielding, he lifted a hand to stroke the side of her face tenderly, and added softly: 'That was what your dream had been about the afternoon you weren't well, wasn't it? "He's so lovely," you said, as if you had no doubts about it being a boy.'

'I saw him so clearly, Bret,' she said softly, feeling his hair thick and vital under her fingers. 'He had dark hair like yours——'

'And yours!'

'——and grey eyes like yours.'

'We'll have other babies, Jinny,' he said huskily, his breath warm against her lips. 'And maybe when their father comes home tired at night, their mother will make him some special tea.'

'She will, Bret,' Jinny smiled mistily. 'Always.'

Harlequin Announces the
COLLECTION EDITIONS
OF 1978

stories of special
beauty and significance

25 Beautiful stories of particular merit

In 1976 we introduced the first 100 Harlequin Collections — a selection of titles chosen from our best sellers of the past 20 years. This series, a trip down memory lane, proved how great romantic fiction can be timeless and appealing from generation to generation. Perhaps because the theme of love and romance is eternal, and, when placed in the hands of talented, creative, authors whose true gift lies in their ability to write from the heart, the stories reach a special level of brilliance that the passage of time cannot dim. Like a treasured heirloom, an antique of superb craftsmanship, a beautiful gift from someone loved, — these stories too, have a special significance that transcends the ordinary.

Here's your 1978 Harlequin Collection Editions . . .

More great Harlequin 1978 Collection Editions . . .

122 Moon Over Africa
Pamela Kent
(#983)

123 Island In The Dawn
Averil Ives
(#984)

124 Lady In Harley Street
Anne Vinton
(#985)

125 Play The Tune Softly
Amanda Doyle
(#1116)

126 Will You Surrender?
Joyce Dingwell
(#1179)

Original Harlequin Romance numbers in brackets